# A RUN FOR THE MYSTIC

## SHADY GROVE PSYCHIC MYSTERIES
### BOOK 8

## ADA BELL

EMPRESS BOOKS

# ALSO BY ADA BELL

**Shady Grove Psychic Mysteries**

Mystic Pieces

The Scry's the Limit

Sight Seering

Seer Today, Gone Tomorrow

The Pie in the Scry

Mystic Persons

The Psychic's the Thing

A Run for the Mystic

Election Seer

**Shady Grove Novellas**

Mystic Treasure (Book 3.5)

8 Maids a-Meddling (Book 9.5)

**Haunted Haven Series**

Unfinished Witchness

Risky Witchness

Open for Witchness

Murder on the Witch Express (Spring 2025)

**Bundles and Boxed Sets**

Shady Grove Psychic Mysteries 1-3

Shady Grove Psychic Mysteries 4-6

Shady Grove Psychic Mysteries 1-6: The Katrina Conundrum

Haunted Haven Mysteries 1-3

# PRAISE FOR ADA BELL

"*Mystic Pieces* is a charming, humorous, and original mystery that weaves a tale of murder and self-discovery with heart, family, and psychic visions."

*READERS' FAVORITE*

"...I liked Aly as a main character and reading about her and her powers. I liked the side characters and how each had their own personality that made it easy to remember. All in all I really enjoyed this book and look forward to the next book in the series!"

LOLA'S BOOK REVIEWS

"A cute and cozy introduction to the quirky and devoted characters, *Mystic Pieces* is the perfect first installment to the Shady Grove Psychic Mystery Series."

LITERARY LIONESS

The attached novel is a work of fiction. Any resemblance to actual persons, places, or events is merely a coincidence.

Copyright © 2024 by Ada Bell. Cover image by Victoria Cooper Art. Mystic crystal ball image ©2020 by simply whyte design. Used with permission.

All rights reserved. No part of this book may be reproduced in any form or by any means without the prior written consent of the Publisher, except brief quotes used in reviews.

Empress Books

P.O. Box 1572

Clifton Park, NY 12065

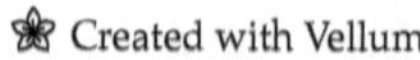 Created with Vellum

*To Sharon.*
*If Aly had a horse, she would absolutely name him*
*Sir Isaac Newton.*

# PROLOGUE

THE NIGHT STARTED COMPLETELY NORMAL, at least by Shady Grove's standards. Saturday was my regular closing shift at the antique store, which stayed pleasantly busy most of the day. My boss, Olive, and I had been happily chatting about my plans to visit the racetrack with my boyfriend tomorrow while unloading boxes donated by a local resident. When Olive discovered I didn't know what to wear, she'd volunteered to lend me an outfit.

After Olive left to find me a dress, I'd found a mysteriously glowing necklace. Although I'd learned about my psychic powers almost a year and a half ago, I'd never seen anything like this. Magical jewelry was the last thing I expected to find sorting donations from a regular family.

If it hadn't been shining with a pearly white light, the necklace would have been downright uninteresting. A simple string of white seashells, woven together by strands of thick black thread. It didn't look expensive. A regular person would have chucked it into the costume jewelry, never to be seen again.

But I couldn't do that. Not when the necklace called to me so strongly. My mom had long stressed the importance of using my psychic powers to help people, and this necklace wanted to share its knowledge.

First, I needed to verify that it wasn't dangerous. I called Olive, my voice quiet and shaky. I tried again, louder.

"Aly? What's wrong?" She re-entered carrying a pink dress with matching jacket on a hanger and holding a feathered hat. "What's in that box, a snake?"

When I spoke, my voice came out hushed, as if speaking too loudly would anger the mystical item. "That's why I called you. I have no idea."

She peeked inside the box. "It's just a necklace. Did it give you a vision?"

"I'm afraid to pick it up. I was hoping you'd know why it's glowing and what it means."

"It probably wants you to wear it."

"Yeah, no. I don't think so," I said.

"You've never been injured during a vision, have you?" Olive asked.

"There's a first time for everything."

"True, but I think you're safe."

I took a deep breath. "Do you see what I'm seeing?"

"I see a puka shell necklace. I don't know why it's here. These things aren't valuable. It's sitting on top of some folded clothes."

"Is that it?"

She turned her head back and forth, her eyes glued to the interior of the box. "Out the corner of my eye, it glows, but not when I look directly."

"Can you tell me who owns it?"

My boss's antique store did well because she had a psychic ability to know who truly owned an item. People were always happy with their purchases. I expected her to reach for the necklace, but she didn't.

"Sure. Tripp wore this necklace every day in high school. They were extremely popular. Everyone had them."

"Are you absolutely positive this was his?"

"You know, identifying a twenty-year-old necklace without magic is actually more impressive," Olive grumbled, reaching into the box. "But yes, this belongs to Tripp."

"Do you get anything else from it?"

"Nothing that should stop you from trying it on. It's asking for you."

I held out my hands. "Okay, then. Lay it on me."

Olive placed the necklace over my head. As it settled into place, she vanished.

*I stood on the doorstep of a large Victorian house. Three college guys welcomed me from the doorway.*

*"It's okay, man," said someone next to me. "Be cool."*

Until he spoke, I hadn't noticed this guy. *He was shorter than me and muscular, with sun-streaked blonde hair and a dark tan. Everyone looked around my age.*

*Clenching my jaw, I nodded. "Let's get a drink."*

*Inside, a party raged. Music blared from a dimly lit room to the left of the front hallway. Dancing students filled the space. Across the hall, a pretty girl with long blonde curls and blue eyes glared at two girls nearby. One of them, a pale-faced brunette, looked oddly familiar. The other held a trophy or something, but I didn't get a good look. When the first girl saw me watching, she said something to her friends. They fled through a doorway behind them.*

*My friend led me through away from the girls, using what looked like a fencing sword to create a path through the crowd. When we reached the kitchen, someone put a drink in my hand. It tasted sweet, something sugary masking the taste of cheap gin. I hated cheap gin, but anything to dull the pain. I downed half of it in one gulp.*

Everything blurred. When my vision became clear again, I stood in a different room.

*Now I held another drink, this one full.* With interest, I noted my tanned hands, several shades darker than my usual complexion. The hands were bigger than mine. *On my left wrist, I wore a bracelet matching the puka shell necklace and my right hand had a big class ring with a giant K on the top.*

*Tripp Kavanaugh.*

*People packed into this room, dancing to music so loud, conversation was impossible. In the low lights, I struggled to navigate without walking into people. My stomach churned. Sword Guy had vanished, but the blonde from before stood near the staircases, looking around like she was waiting for someone. A clock on the wall read just after midnight.*

*I approached her and smiled. My voice was low, deep. "Hey, Penny. How you doing?"*

*"I'm fine. Enjoy the rest of the party, Tripp. I'm leaving." She turned away, but I stopped her.*

*"Where are you going?" My words came out slurred. I stumbled against the wall. "Are you waiting for someone?"*

*"It's none of your business." Penny sighed. "You're drunk."*

*"I'm fine. I just need…" The room spun. "To lie down."*

*She looked around as if needing help before putting her arm around my waist. "Let's get you upstairs."*

*Everything blurred again.*

*I lay on something soft. A bed! My shorts and T-shirt were on the floor. Something soft draped over me. A blanket. Oh, soft blanket. My mouth felt like I'd swallowed a raccoon. Someone moved, reminding me I wasn't alone.*

*Groaning, I opened my eyes to see Penny standing over me.*

*I gripped her hand. "Stay with me? Just for a minute."*

*She sighed. "Fine. My ride probably left by now, anyway. I'll wait until you're okay. But Tripp, this has to stop. We're over."*

*"Thank you." I grabbed the cup off the table and chugged the water, then leaned back. "I'm really sorry about how things ended."*

*She smiled briefly. "So am I."*

*Everything went dark.*

*Sometime later, I opened my eyes. The house was quiet. Bright light streamed into the room.*

*Throwing back the blankets, I sat up. My head pounded. I needed water, greasy food, and a bathroom. Not necessarily in that order.*

*Penny must have refilled the glass on the nightstand after I fell asleep. I guzzled the water, barely noticing how much liquid sloshed down my chest. After drinking the last drop, I felt okay to get up.*

*The wooden floor was cold beneath my bare feet. Someone screamed. I winced.*

*"Tripp! What did you do, man?" a male voice said.*

*Me? I fell asleep, I woke up…*

*"What are you talking about?" I turned toward the door.*

*—and found Penny in the bed.*

*Briefly, hope rose that we'd made up despite my drunken stupor. That didn't explain the screaming. Then I noticed the angle of her head, how her limbs splayed. Her beautiful blue eyes, staring sightlessly at the ceiling. And blood everywhere. So much blood.*

*Penny was dead.*

I yanked the necklace over my head and dropped it like it burned. Leaning back against the wall, I gasped. "Water."

Olive ran out and returned with a cup seconds later. I sipped gratefully before she led me to a chair. The images replayed in my mind on a loop. I inhaled through my nose and exhaled through my mouth, counting each breath until I felt human.

"That was intense."

"Are you okay?" Olive asked. "What did you see?"

"A girl was murdered."

Her eyes widened. "Did you see Tripp do it?"

"Not exactly." My eyes narrowed. "Hold on. How do you know what I saw?"

"This is Tripp Kavanaugh's necklace. He was convicted of murdering Penny, his ex-girlfriend, in 1997." Her voice cracked before she composed herself. "It would be strange if anything previously belonging to the Kavanaughs gave you a vision of someone else's death."

I nodded. "Did you know her?"

"Everyone knew Penny Langley. Tripp, too. We were the same age."

"You were in high school in 1997?" My voice gave away my confusion. "How old are you?"

Olive put her hands on her hips. "How old do you *think* I am?"

My mind raced for a non-offensive answer. "Uh, thirty-seven?"

She twisted her lips. "Nice try. You think Sam was born when I was in junior high? How old do you think I am?"

I avoided her gaze. "Well, um, when we first met, you were wearing that old-time costume. Then, I don't know… everyone older than me looks around fifty until they hit retirement age."

"Fifty!" She gasped. "You're lucky you're my favorite employee."

I refrained from pointing out that she'd never had other employees, only occasional help from her son. Instead, I asked, "What happened after Penny died?"

"Oh, you know how it is. The police immediately zeroed in on Tripp. He couldn't give an alibi but swore he didn't know how she died. A jury disagreed."

A frat party explained why the house looked both familiar and not. Those houses had been on campus forever. My former roommate dragged me to a couple of parties over the years; chances were I'd been there. Then the second part of Olive's statement sank in. "If Tripp owned this necklace, he might have been telling the truth. I didn't see her death. Either he didn't do it or he was too drunk to remember."

"That was his defense," she said. "It didn't pan out."

In the time I'd known Olive, we'd discussed many murders. Never had she seemed affected by one. "How well did you know them?"

"We were passing acquaintances, I guess. I wasn't close to either of them. Penny and Tripp went to private schools, but I'd run into them during the holidays. I was actually at the party, although I didn't stay long."

"Wait. You were there?" I asked incredulously. "Way to bury the lede."

"I wasn't a witness. I went home long before Penny died.

Everything I know came from someone else," she said. "What did you see?"

"It's choppy." Closing my eyes, I replayed the scenes from the vision. "They were at a party. It was definitely ages ago, because they were dancing to grocery store music. Tripp wore a bracelet that matches this necklace."

Olive bit her lip before she replied. "First, grocery stores play excellent music. Second, what do you mean by choppy?"

"Everything came in pieces. I think the events were in order, but I jumped around to different rooms. It was like three memories jammed into one. Is that possible?"

"I've never seen it happen, but I suppose with strong enough emotions, it could."

"Tripp definitely had a mess of feelings. He wanted to talk to Penny." Another thought struck me. "Could parts of a vision be erased?"

Her nose wrinkled as she considered the question. "A powerful witch can cleanse an item. You've seen that before. But to remove parts of a vision? Why?"

"To cover up a murder. I saw Penny, but I don't know what happened to her. What if Tripp remembered the murder originally and someone removed it from the necklace?"

"Seems like a lot of trouble," she said. "What good would wiping the necklace do? It wouldn't erase Tripp's memories. And erasing his memory shouldn't affect the imprint on the necklace."

"Yeah." I sighed. "Excellent point."

"Tripp drank heavily that night. The alcohol could've contributed to the problem."

"True. He was slurring his speech and had trouble walking. When he woke up, he didn't know where he was."

"Maybe some memories never imprinted because of his blood alcohol content," Olive said.

Was it a total coincidence that this necklace wound up here with me?

"Do you think Lucretia knew this message held a vision?" I asked.

"It's hard to say. If Lucretia doesn't have magic, this would seem like an ordinary necklace." She picked up the necklace from where I'd dropped it, examining it with exaggerated care. "Cute, huh?"

"Is that really what you think?"

"Of course not." Olive grinned at me. "When Lucretia and I discussed the donation, she mentioned having mixed feelings about giving away Tripp's things. All this time, she'd hoped to find evidence of her son's innocence that the police overlooked."

"You told her about me!" I was more intrigued than outraged, and we both knew it. "Olive, my powers are supposed to be secret."

She shrugged. "It's a small town; people talk. Everyone knows you've solved several murders the police couldn't. There have been whispers. I only dropped a couple of hints. Lucretia hoped something in all this junk would inspire you to investigate."

"After twenty years?"

"Tripp maintains his innocence still. Every day in prison must be excruciating, especially for an innocent person. If he didn't do it, he deserves to be released."

"Do you think his family is desperate enough to consult a psychic?"

"She might be." Olive's eyes flashed with excitement. "Aly, do you know what this means? After all these years, you might uncover the truth!"

# CHAPTER ONE

AFTER GETTING HIT with Tripp's memories, I didn't have the energy to keep unpacking boxes. Olive assured me we'd made enough progress for one day. We weren't hurting for inventory.

My boyfriend, Cal, and I had to get up early for a race-track tour in the morning, so after Olive packed the necklace away, I tried on the dress she'd brought me, which I'd forgotten about entirely. It fit, so I went home, not even noticing the details. The vision stayed with me.

In June, I'd moved into Rusty and Doug's house. My college roommate graduated and moved to California, and I couldn't stand the thought of living with a stranger. My part-time job didn't pay enough to rent an apartment, so Rusty and Doug offered to let me use their guest room, at least for the summer. When I arrived, I greeted them in a daze and went to my room, my brain still processing.

Olive had known Penny and Tripp. The police investigated in 1997. The evidence pointed at Tripp, despite what Lucretia believed. However, Olive's excitement at my vision suggested she also thought he was innocent. After all, if he'd done it, everyone already knew the truth.

Olive wouldn't intentionally sway my opinion but hadn't concealed her feelings well. If I could exonerate Tripp, didn't I have an obligation to try?

On the other hand, Tripp Kavanaugh was convicted by a jury of his peers. For all I knew, the police already discovered what happened. Justice for Penny had been done, hadn't it? Everyone's mom thought they were innocent. No one wanted to believe their child could kill someone.

So what happened to Penny?

Tripp had indisputably been at the frat house the night of Penny's murder. He was in the room when she'd died, unless someone planted her in the bed.

Unfortunately, my vision skipped the crucial part of the timeline. I had no idea who killed Penny. For all I knew, an alternate personality took control of Tripp during the parts of the vision I couldn't view.

My brother, Kevin, had studied this case in law school. When Mrs. Kavanaugh's donation first came into the store, I'd mentioned it in passing. Kevin said Tripp's defense was "I don't remember killing Penny." Essentially, he was so drunk, he didn't know whether he'd murdered her. That didn't instill much confidence in me. Or the jury, it turned out. Not remembering didn't mean he didn't do it.

As I got ready for bed, I shoved those thoughts out of my head. Where would I start investigating a murder from so long ago? Not to mention, poking my nose where it didn't belong almost got me killed last spring. Someone tried to burn Missing Pieces down. Maybe I should focus on myself and leave other people's problems alone. Spend more time with Cal and look at our future rather than the past.

A voice sounding suspiciously like my mom echoed in the back of my head. "Aly, your powers are a gift. Helping others is how you thank the powers that be for granting them."

A groan escaped me. Mom wasn't here, but my conscience could use her to guilt me. Unfortunately, she was right. I had an obligation to help people. If Tripp didn't kill Penny, he didn't deserve to have his life taken, and Penny hadn't received justice.

After what felt like hours, I fell into a restless doze.

My alarm rang much too early on Sunday morning. Cal's cousin had arranged for us to get a behind-the-scenes tour of the racetrack starting at seven. It seemed like a great idea when I'd expected to be awake. Now I wondered why Jacob hated us.

A long shower and coffee helped me feel more human. In all the commotion caused by my vision last night, I'd almost forgotten to take the loaned outfit home, but now I dressed in a knee-length pink sheath dress with matching jacket and high heels. A fabulous feather and a white flower adorned the enormous hat. To complete the look, Olive had also given me a matching white belt and pink clutch, each with a flower. Last night, I'd barely noticed how gorgeous this fabric was, the way the silky material slid over my hips, or the jaunty tilt to the purple feather. I looked awesome. Slowly, excitement overtook my exhaustion.

The racetrack on the edge of Shady Grove County was one of the area's most touted tourist destinations. I'd never been, but Cal's family loved it. They'd attended every season for years.

When we arrived, Cal drove all the way to the front of the massive parking lot, bypassing about a thousand parked cars. As soon as an empty space came into view, I jabbed my finger at the window. "There! Stop!"

"Oh, no. We're VIPs, remember?"

Jacob's invitation had included the VIP tour, grandstand seats, and free admission to the buffet. Those things I remembered. Grad students never turned down a free meal. I hadn't realized we'd get parking, too.

Cal bypassed a valet stand and turned into a VIP lot near the main entrance. We were a quarter of a mile closer than the parking space I found.

"Fancy!" I said.

He grinned. "Stick with me. We're going places. Today, at least."

Walking up to the gates, I felt incredibly grateful for Olive's help finding something to wear. With my dress and Cal's seersucker suit and straw hat, we fit right in. A few people wore shorts and T-shirts, but most women milling around near the grandstand sported outfits not that different from mine.

And the hats! Olive was right about the hats, too. Suddenly, mine seemed less flamboyant and almost boring. Still, I loved it.

Having never been to a racetrack, I didn't expect the vibrance of the crowd, the excitement filling the air. To my left, people lined up in front of betting windows. Huge boards behind the track showed a chart that probably would explain the odds if I knew how to read it. Nearby lay bleachers, which were already filling up, though the races wouldn't start for hours.

Beside me, Cal took in everything through the lens of a state-of-the-art camera he'd gotten for his birthday. It had multiple lenses, a special carrying case, and a detachable flash. His work had been improving steadily over the past several weeks.

He clicked away, looking blissful.

"Where's your cousin?" I asked.

"We'll see him later. The jockeys aren't part of the VIP tour." He pointed to a small shuttle bus. "There's our ride."

"We need a ride?"

"Oh, yeah. The stables are way over there." Cal gestured toward the far side of the track.

I followed him into the small vehicle and took a seat, noting about half a dozen people already aboard.

As we trundled toward the tour's starting point, Cal pointed out the box seats, the paddock, the grandstand, the bathrooms, and more. Then we stopped in front of a stable, one of many similar structures tucked out of sight of the seats.

Our tour guide waited at the entrance of the stable to our right, greeting everyone with a smile as we disembarked.

The introduction to racing passed in a flurry of information. According to our guide, the track stables held more than a thousand stalls. We saw several horses worth more than my brother's four-bedroom house. (All the racing Thoroughbreds were male, I discovered. How sexist.) The stable employed thousands of people, including jockeys, groomers, trainers, and farriers, who I was disappointed to learn did not transport horses back and forth on a boat. Apparently, it involved shoes.

The track even housed employees. Cool. We peeked inside one room. Except for the lack of desks, it reminded me of the college dorm I'd vacated in June. Small, functional, not luxurious. It beat paying Saratoga summer rent, though.

Our tour ended in the stable where we'd begun. The guide ended his speech and asked if anyone had questions. We'd nearly finished when a clang ripped through the air. Everyone turned.

Behind us, a short blonde woman glared red-faced at the ground. She wore a bright green silk shirt and white riding pants with very shiny boots. A bucket lay a couple of feet away from her. When she spotted the group, she froze.

Our tour guide didn't miss a beat. "Here is one of our jockeys now, Morgan Gunderson! Maybe Morgan can tell us…"

Before he could finish, the jockey stormed off. The tour guide swallowed, looking around. "Stable workers use these buckets for general maintenance and cleaning! Let's move on. Here's one of our trainers, Ryder Jennings! Say hello to Ryder, everyone!"

A tall, broad-shouldered man with black hair and freckled,

pale skin stepped into the light, lips pressed together. He wore work clothes, much like the others we'd seen walking around the area. Everyone except the jockeys, anyway.

He raised one hand in a wave. "Uh, hey! I hope you're enjoying the tour."

The group cheered.

"Ryder, what can you tell us about the racing business?" our guide asked.

"First, I want to confirm: yes, my name is Ryder, and I train horses for a living," he said with a wide smile. "My mom wasn't psychic, but let's say she was hopeful. She started me on lessons when I was four."

"It must be exciting to watch one of your horses win," our tour guide continued. "Ryder's trained several champions. What's the secret to your success?"

"Oh, you know. The horses need to know who's boss. Show 'em a firm hand; don't use the whip unless they ask for it. Like a woman."

Ew.

Behind me, a woman gasped.

"What a jerk," Cal whispered.

Perhaps Ryder realized we'd cooled to his presence, because he rubbed the back of his neck and looked toward the door. "If you'll excuse me, I'm running late."

He rushed through the door the jockey had used.

Our guide smiled broadly in an unsuccessful effort to hide his flusteration. "There you have it, folks! Never a dull moment. Let's take the bus to the front gate."

When we exited the stable, the sun had climbed over the horizon, making temperatures rise. Already, humidity hung thick in the air. Those poor horses. Today wasn't a nice day for running.

Of course, in my opinion, no weather would make running with a person on my back less torturous.

Following the rest of the group, I started to board the bus. Cal pulled me back. "Not us. We're staying here."

The guide approached. Cal flashed our VIP badges, and he nodded. "Enjoy your day."

"What's next?" I asked after the bus drove away.

"Over there." Cal nodded toward a short guy standing near a small outdoor ring. "Jake is going to show us things not on the public tour."

Most of Cal's extended family lived in Saratoga, but Jacob traveled where the job took him. We'd never met. Still, the guy waiting for our arrival was unmistakably a member of the Brunner family. The newcomer had shaved his hair on the sides, leaving the top long, but he and my boyfriend shared the same pale skin, generous smiles, and friendly brown eyes. Cal towered over his cousin, but otherwise, they could be twins.

Jacob wore a bright red silk shirt with matching cap and pristine white pants. Other than the color, his outfit matched the jockey from the tour.

"Hey, man!" Cal greeted him with a high-five before turning to me. "Aly, this is Jake."

"Nice to meet you, Jake," I said.

"Jacob is fine," he said, glaring at his cousin. "Only people I don't like call me Jake."

After having many similar conversations with my brother over the years, the family teasing put me at ease. I glanced at Cal. "What do you think? Do I want him to like me?"

Jacob chuckled. "I like her already. Are you ready for the non-public tour?"

"Is there food?" The question leaped out of my mouth before I could stop to think. My cheeks burned. "Sorry. I've been awake for ages."

"You'll have a much more attentive audience if we eat first," Cal said.

Jacob nodded toward a clock on the wall behind us. "Sorry, the buffet isn't open yet. I'll make it quick. We'll just say hello to the first horse I'm racing today."

"I can't believe you get to ride here. Who'd you knock off?" Cal asked.

"Shh! Don't let the others hear you!" Jacob looked around with exaggerated concern. To me, he said, "Mr. Hill hired me as a stable hand years ago while I trained as a jockey. He's like a father to me. He'd talked about letting me ride this season, but another jockey had seniority. Then Bryce was in an accident, and I got the call."

"What happened? Is horse racing dangerous?" I asked. Although I'd only known Jacob for about forty seconds, Cal would be devastated if anything happened to his favorite cousin.

"Not if you stay on top of the horse!" Jacob's smile faded. "I'm joking. Yes, you have to be careful when riding, especially at these speeds. But we've had years of training. Bryce is an excellent rider. He was in a car accident last night after leaving the track."

"That sucks. Is he okay?" Cal asked.

"He's fine," Jacob said. "Broke a leg."

While we chatted, he led us through the stable, past more horses, all of them impeccably groomed and utterly gorgeous. Several stuck their noses out of the stalls to say hello as we walked past. Not for the first time, I wished I'd taken horseback riding lessons as a child.

Soon Jacob stopped in front of a stall holding a gorgeous brown horse with a black mane and tail. "This is Speed Racer."

"Nice to meet you," I said as the horse sniffed in my direction. "Can I pet him?"

"Sure."

Reaching out, I stroked the horse's soft nose. It sneezed and turned away. I laughed. "Apparently, I've been dismissed."

"Beautiful horse," Cal said, raising the black backpack holding his camera. "Can I take a few shots?"

"Not in here. Once we're outside, sure." Jacob gestured around. "The owners get weird about it if you're not press."

"No problem," Cal said.

"This is all so glamorous," I said. "How do you become a jockey?"

"Well, first you've got to learn to ride." Jacob elbowed his cousin. "That's why Cal couldn't do it."

"Ouch," Cal said.

"Is that it? You learn to ride really well, and then you try out?" I asked.

"I wish! They hired me to muck out stalls, then I moved to groom. I went to jockey school, but it's not required. Before you can race, you have to earn a license. It's a long process."

"Jake has been working up to jockey for years," Cal said proudly.

I was about to ask how to get a license without jockey school when the red-faced girl from earlier stomped over. Her demeanor hadn't improved.

When she spotted the three of us, she sneered. "Bringing the family to work on your first day?"

"Can I help you, Morgan?" To me and Cal, Jacob said, "Morgan rides for Mr. Hill, too. She's in a few races today."

"You can tell me what happened to Bryce," Morgan demanded. "You're not supposed to be here."

"Yes, I am honored to fill in. Thank you for your kind words," Jacob said sarcastically. "When Mr. Hill calls, I answer. If you want to know what happened to Bryce, ask him."

"I did," she said. "We spoke this morning, and I'm not sure the collision was an accident."

I gasped.

Morgan glanced over, noticing me for the first time. "Don't you think it's suspicious that he got hurt right after the season opened? After you trained so hard and he got the final jockey spot? Where were you after the races yesterday, anyway?"

Cal stepped forward, putting himself between them. He turned toward Morgan, towering over her. At six-foot-three, he could be quite intimidating when he wanted (which wasn't often). "What are you trying to say?"

The blood drained from Morgan's face. She stepped backward, swallowing. Then she leaned around Cal to look at Jacob. "This isn't over. You're going to be sorry."

# CHAPTER TWO

IN SILENCE, we watched Morgan storm off for the second time that morning. Once she moved out of sight, Jacob muttered, "If I got to break someone's legs, I'd pick yours."

I snorted.

Cal shot him a worried look. "Do you want us to stick around in case she comes back?"

"No, thanks. Morgan wouldn't hurt me. She's just nervous about the races."

"I'd think to people who've worked here awhile, jockeying would be old hat," I said.

"I'll let you know if that happens." He winked at me. "But for some of us, the nerves are always there. The key is to work past them. Morgan's horse in our race is favored to win, and that's a lot of pressure."

"What about you and Speed Racer here?" Cal asked.

"He's a long shot, but I'm going to try to make the family proud."

"You already have." Cal fist-bumped him.

"Thanks, man." Jacob glanced at a clock on the far wall. "Sorry to kick you out, but Speed Racer needs to warm up. Besides, the buffet opens soon."

It would take at least fifteen minutes to get back to the private clubhouse from the stables. Fancy clothes made me walk slower than usual, the shuttle bus was long gone, and the stables stood a long way from the public racetrack.

We wished Jacob luck and left.

When the betting windows came into view, Cal nodded toward them. "I'm going to put twenty bucks on Speed Racer. For Jake."

"Great idea!" I pulled my wallet out of my bag. "Me, too."

He waved me away. "You're my guest. I'll get us both, and if Jake wins, we'll split the money."

"Thanks. I'll wait here." The lines at the betting window were long, and my feet already protested standing in Maria's dress shoes all morning. They matched the outfit beautifully, but I longed for a pair of beaten-up old sneakers.

Once Cal got in line, I approached the fence separating the spectators from the racetrack where several horses were warming up. I raised a hand to wave to Speed Racer, then stopped when I caught sight of the rider's curly brown hair and dark complexion. That wasn't Jacob.

Now that I thought about it, none of the people on the field looked like jockeys. No shiny shirts with matching hats, and some of them were pretty tall. The track probably had people to warm up the horses before the event started. Maybe it was a step toward becoming a professional jockey.

A flash of familiar red hair near the rail caught my eye. Not auburn like Cal; a bright coppery red. Creeping closer, I peeked out from under my hat. Sure enough, the *Shady Grove Sentinel* newspaper's premier—and by that, I meant only—reporter leaned up against the railing.

What was TJ Crews doing here? Sports reporting seemed like the kind of thing he considered beneath him.

In an alternate universe, TJ had a history of making up news stories when reality wasn't interesting enough. He'd practically accused me of murder once. Sure, he didn't remember it, but I did. He better not be planning a hatchet job on the jockeys. Jacob didn't need TJ to ruin his racing debut with lies.

Thankfully, he hadn't noticed me. We barely knew each other in this reality, but the rumor mill suggested he still wasn't above embellishing the facts to get more traffic to the paper's website. After I solved a murder at the college last spring, he'd written an in-depth article asking how I knew so much and insinuating that I had a "magic touch."

Yes, that happened to be true, but I didn't want everyone to know.

"Aly!" someone called.

Given the commonality of my nickname, I ignored the voice and started toward the clubhouse.

"Aluminum Reynolds!"

That one brought me to a halt. Darn it. Why had my parents given me such a distinctive name?

Gritting my teeth, I forced a smile and turned. "Hello, TJ."

"Listen, I'm glad I ran into you. It's nice to see a familiar face."

"Why? Was there a crime at the track you need to pin on an innocent party?"

He laughed a shade too loudly. "Dad wanted a puff piece about the racetrack. The history, the special events, all that jazz. He thinks people around here will be interested."

"You must be bored out of your mind."

"You're not wrong," TJ said. "But duty calls. What are you doing here?"

"I came to watch the races. My boyfriend is placing a bet right now."

There was no reason to mention Jacob. While some jockeys might love snagging a reporter's attention, I wouldn't sic TJ on my worst enemy. If his father didn't own the paper, TJ would have been fired years ago.

"Oh, yeah?" TJ raised one eyebrow. "Are you a gambler, then?"

"Absolutely! I love putting down money on the sports and

hoping it comes back to me." Why did my mouth wrestle control from my brain whenever I lied? TJ would never believe my gibberish. Still, I gritted my teeth and hung onto my smile.

"Right." He shifted for a minute, then leaned forward. "Did anyone give you a message for me?"

"Um, no. Why?"

"Never mind. You should go. No reason to poke your nose into matters that don't concern you."

Was TJ writing something more sinister than a puff piece? No, he was probably trying to make himself sound important by dropping obscure hints. "I'm here to watch the races. And in case you were wondering, I'm not going to magic any of the horses into first place."

His jaw clenched, but he didn't reply. I was about to leave when he looked me in the eye. "Aly, I'm serious. Everyone knows you like to play detective. Don't get involved with this."

The fear in his eyes made me shiver. I'd seen cocky TJ, arrogant TJ, and annoying TJ. Never had I seen him afraid. To my knowledge, horse racing wasn't inherently dangerous—at least, not for the spectators. What caused this change of character?

A thought hit me like a bolt of lightning. Maybe Morgan was right, and a car accident hadn't been the reason Bryce couldn't race. TJ might know more about what happened last night.

Well, if that was the case, TJ and the police were welcome to figure it out. I'd come for a fun day with my boyfriend and nothing else.

"I promise I'm just here to enjoy the races," I said before walking away.

The whole way to the clubhouse, it felt like someone was watching me. I tried to convince myself to ignore it, but my uneasiness grew with each step. When I got to the building, I spun around.

No one was there. The crowds had swallowed TJ. But I still felt unseen eyes on my back.

# CHAPTER THREE

NEAR THE BUFFET, Cal greeted me with a big smile and a clean plate. Happily, I joined him, taking in the scrambled eggs, bacon, sliced ham, waffles, melon, and more. Farther down, I spied cooked salmon, grilled zucchini, and even a beef carving station. My mouth watered.

Like any respectable grad student, I never let a free meal go to waste. Rolling up my sleeves, I vowed to see how much food I could squirrel away. We'd be here for hours.

After piling my plate high, I followed Cal to a table near the front of the room. Massive windows covered this entire wall. I gasped. Although I'd known this building stood near the track, the horses were so close I could practically touch them.

"Beautiful, isn't it?" Cal said. "Wait until you see them fly by."

"When do the races start?" I asked.

"A few minutes after one."

"Is that when we'll see Jacob?"

"No, he's in the second race. We'll watch from the grandstand. This place is nice, but there's nothing like experiencing the crowd's excitement."

"You're dying to take that tie off, aren't you?"

"Absolutely." He nodded toward his camera bag, sitting on the chair between us. "I'd also like to shoot some pictures without the window."

"I hope your camera doesn't get drenched." All morning, dark clouds had been inching toward us. "I'm happy to go out there, but if it rains, you're on your own."

He shrugged. "You know these summer storms. It'll end before you find cover."

"So that's why everyone wears hats."

Instead of responding, he stuffed a piece of bacon in his mouth, chewing enthusiastically.

After brunch, we went outside. The grandstand wasn't air-conditioned like the club, but Jacob had reserved a spot in the shade for us. Cal was right. Being in the crowd beat standing behind a window, even in the humidity.

When we took our seats at the top of the grandstand, the first race was about to start. Horses lined up, ready for the signal.

The gun went off, and the animals thundered down the track. Each wore a blanket matching the jockey's outfit. The blankets also showed the number of each horse. That must be how you knew who won. Jacob wasn't riding, so I looked for Morgan, the only other jockey I'd met. No sign of her.

Cal lifted his camera, clicking away.

"Do you want to go closer for Jacob's race?" I asked. "You'll get better pictures."

He grinned and gestured toward the field. "I can see over everyone's heads, and I've got a good zoom."

Having grown up where horse racing wasn't common, I hadn't known what to expect. It was loud, for one thing. The horses' flying hooves kicked up huge plumes of dust. But each horse ran as if his life depended on it. These were powerful machines, operating at peak performance. Their beauty took my breath away. When the winning horse broke the ribbon, I understood why people loved racing.

According to the online program, Jacob would start the

second race in spot number eight. With interest, I noted that he'd be next to Morgan on a horse named Maverick. Speed Racer and Maverick appeared to be approximately the same size. Jacob's mount, according to Cal, was called a bay: brown coat with a black mane, tail, and legs. He didn't know why. Beside Jacob, Morgan rode a dappled gray horse.

The starting gun blasted, and the horses pounded out of the gates. Speed Racer slid through the pack, moving close to the rail like a hot knife cutting butter. Maverick was on his heels. Two other horses crowded around them, so close I couldn't tell where one creature ended and the next began. The pack stayed close for the first lap. They seemed equally matched.

I cheered, hoping to see Jacob beat Morgan, even if she *was* riding the favorite. After the way she'd berated Jacob this morning, winning his first official race would be extra sweet.

As the horses rounded the bend for what Cal called "the home stretch," the crowd went wild. People rose to their feet. Since my view was now blocked, I joined them, craning my neck and clapping. Cal helped me step onto my seat so I could look for Jacob and Speed Racer. We cheered together, clapping and yelling for number eight.

"And the winner is…."

A massive cheer swallowed the rest of the announcement. With no idea who'd won, I popped onto my toes, holding Cal's shoulder for support. I couldn't even tell the horses apart. Cal's smile told me to expect good news, though.

He swept me off the bench into a hug and spun me around. "He did it! Second place!"

"Awesome!" I cheered right along with him. "Who won?"

"Maverick."

Hmmph. It was childish, but part of me felt like someone so rude didn't deserve to win. The horse ran well, though. It wasn't his fault his rider was a jerk.

When the crowd settled, Cal set me back on the ground. On the field, three horses moved toward the winner's circle.

The remaining riders walked their mounts toward a gate on the side facing the stables. I hoped they got tasty snacks and lots of water after working so hard. Both riders and horses deserved it.

Cal and I settled back into our seats. About twenty minutes later, Jacob came in fifth on a horse named Eclipse. It wasn't as exhilarating as watching him almost win, but I loved rooting for someone we knew. Cal took everything in through the lens of his camera, documenting the day.

Before I knew it, the horses lined up for the final race. Again, we'd placed bets on Jacob's mount. We won enough on the first race to cover it, so I felt good about showing my support.

Jacob and the other jockeys mounted their horses, waiting patiently for the gates to rise. Toward the end of the row, I noticed something surprising.

"Why is that spot empty?" I asked Cal, pointing to the second-to-last stall. "Do they not have enough horses?"

"Seems unlikely. Maybe someone pulled out."

"Can't a horse from earlier run again?"

He shook his head emphatically. "Oh, no. No way. They're not allowed to race the same horse more than once a day. The owner would get in big trouble."

The starting signal blew, and I forgot about the empty spot. Jacob's mount, Goose, took an early lead. We clapped and cheered at the top of our lungs, willing him to do well. Jockeys didn't get paid a ton starting out, but every win helped.

At the end of the turn, Goose was nearly a full length ahead. I climbed up onto the seat to urge him along. After seeing Jacob get so close in his first race, we desperately wanted this win.

A quarter lap left. A hundred yards. Ten yards. He did it!

Cal swept me up in a hug that knocked my hat off. We spun around in a circle, still cheering. I threw my head back and laughed before leaning down to kiss him.

"The first blue ribbon!" Cal said.

I beamed at him. "You must be so proud."

By the time Cal got enough pictures of his cousin in the winner's circle, the crowd had begun exiting the grandstand. We waited, letting the bulk of the attendees go ahead rather than get stuck in a hot, sweaty crowd. I didn't know how horses ran in this humidity. The air felt like pea soup.

Once the crowd thinned, we walked back over to the stables to congratulate Jacob on his win.

When the building came into view, an ambulance sat outside. The lights flashed on top, although the siren wasn't blaring.

"Is that normal?" I asked, pointing.

"There are always paramedics here in case someone gets hurt. Vets, too. Even a farrier, in case someone throws a shoe."

"Why would anyone throw their shoe at a horse?"

Cal chuckled, not unkindly. "That's means a horseshoe came off. It's no big deal. Usually there's no need for emergency lights. A few bumps and bruises, nothing serious."

Practically before he'd finished speaking, a police car blasted past us, so close the feather in my hat fluttered. We exchanged a worried look.

"Call Jacob," I said. "I'll hold the camera."

He passed it over and dug into his pocket for his phone. After a moment, he shook his head. "No answer. I'll text."

My pulse raced. First the ambulance, now a police car. Both with lights flashing.

Although the races had ended, the stables remained a beehive of activity. The vibe felt different, though. Maybe people were fatigued from working, but my gut told me something bad happened.

Fear seized me. What if something happened to Jacob? This morning, Morgan was on a rampage. Maybe she'd attacked someone.

"Does this place seem different to you?" Cal asked.

"Definitely."

"Jacob hasn't read my message yet."

"I'm sure he's doing post-race stuff." I squeezed his hand, trying to reassure both of us. He squeezed back, leaving our hands clasped as we approached the stable.

When we drew closer, I discovered another thing that set the building apart from when we'd first seen it. Two security guards stood positioned on either side of the entrance. Earlier, we hadn't passed any bouncers, but now two massive men with blank expressions and dark glasses flanked the door. Each stood with his feet shoulder-width apart, arms crossed against his chest, staring straight ahead.

I approached the man on the left, who was built like a refrigerator. "Hi! We were here earlier. My boyfriend's cousin is a jockey. We wanted to congratulate him on his first win."

"No one goes in or out," he said, staring past me.

"Hold on," Cal said, patting his pockets. "We have VIP badges."

"Employees only," the guard replied. He was even taller than Cal and made of solid muscle. Give this guy some antlers, and he'd double as a moose. "All guest passes are canceled."

The other guard, a man with light brown hair and pinched features, nodded toward the camera still in my hands. Standing next to anyone but his companion, this guy would have been impressively large. His forearms were bigger than my head. "And no pictures."

"What happened?" I asked, nodding toward the ambulance. "Is everyone okay?"

The first guard said, "No comment. We both have no comment."

"My cousin is a jockey," Cal told them again. "I need to know if he's okay."

"Then I suggest you turn your ringer up," Guard 2 said.

"Come on, man! I know he's in there." Cal pitched his voice toward the building. "Jake! Has anyone seen Jacob?"

Both guards stepped forward. I yanked Cal backward.

"Stop!" Jacob's voice made everyone freeze. "Guys, it's okay. They're with me."

When Cal recognized his cousin's voice, he sagged with relief. The guards moved away. I kept my hold on Cal so he wouldn't rush forward again and get into trouble.

Jacob stood in the stable's door looking like he'd seen a ghost.

"Are you okay?" I asked. "What happened?"

Jacob took three steps forward before his knees buckled. He sagged against the wall. Cal rushed toward him, but the security guards got there first to keep Jacob on his feet. "Morgan."

"Did she attack you?" Cal asked. "You look like Goose rode you down the track."

Thunder cracked overhead, shaking the building. Lightning split the air.

"Naw, man. She's dead."

# CHAPTER FOUR

A SECOND CRASH of thunder punctuated Jacob's announcement. Lightning flashed before the rumble faded. These storms rolled in fast. Before anyone could react, the skies opened, dumping the promised shower down as if emptying a bucket onto our heads.

The security guards backed under the eaves, keeping their posts but using the building for cover. Cal pulled me and Jacob under an awning near the training ring. Behind him, rain filled our footprints, washing the area clean.

No one spoke. Jacob's words hung in the air. My moment of relief at finding him unharmed evaporated.

"Morgan's dead? How?" Even shouting, I barely heard myself.

"Are you sure?" Cal asked.

"One hundred percent. I saw her." Jacob closed his eyes to ward off the image. "She's definitely dead."

"That's horrible," I said. "I'm so sorry."

"What happened?" Cal asked.

"She was scheduled to run the last race. When we lined up, her spot was empty. No one knew where she went."

"Did you look for her?"

"No, why? One fewer racer improves everyone's odds. It

wasn't our job to find her." He swallowed and blinked rapidly. "They told me after. She was in Wind Walker's stall."

"Did the horse kill her?" I asked.

"No. This was no accident. There was a hoof pick lying beside her, covered in blood. Someone murdered Morgan."

I gasped.

Cal wrapped the shorter man into a hug. "I'm sorry, Cuz. Listen, it's going to be okay."

"It's not! She's dead and someone killed her and… I don't understand. Five hours ago, she was calling me a jerk."

Cal and I exchanged a look over Jacob's head. If someone murdered Morgan, their argument didn't look good.

Instead of mentioning my concern, I asked, "What's a hoof pick?"

"It's for cleaning horses' hooves," Cal said. "They're very common. Every stable has them."

In my mind's eye, I saw someone cleaning a horse's foot with a small wooden stick. "Isn't that tiny? Like a toothpick?" Two or three inches, like a millimeter wide, and made of brittle wood. Extremely breakable. "How could that kill someone?"

"It's not like a toothpick," Jacob said. "They're sharp. More like a tiny pickaxe. When I was a kid, *someone* dropped one on the floor. I stepped on it. It cut through my shoe into my foot. I needed four stitches."

"Jake, I said I was sorry a billion times," Cal said. At my curious look, he added, "I was five. The stable owners had a dog, and I got distracted. It's no excuse, I know. I should've been more careful. My mom spent a couple of hours loudly explaining my failures that night. Besides, Jake got his revenge the next summer when he made me crash my bike."

"You fell on top of me and broke my right arm."

"Serves you right," Cal said. "You're left-handed; you were fine. Anyway, Aly, a hoof pick in the wrong hands is lethal."

What a nightmare. Poor Jacob. Poor Morgan.

A uniformed police officer stepped out of the stable and spoke to the security guards near the door. Shady Grove only employed two full-time police officers, and this man was neither. They must have asked for help from another county.

The smaller security guard nodded toward the three of us.

"I think the police are ready for your statement," I said.

"Okay, yeah. I'll see you guys later."

"Do you want me to drive you home?" Cal asked. "You shouldn't be alone. Aly can follow us."

"No, I'm fine. Or I will be. Go ahead. I'll text you later."

"You want to get a drink tonight?"

"I don't know. We'll see."

We remained under the awning after Jacob walked away. Despite his assurances, I wasn't confident he could drive safely.

The guards still side-eyed us. I shook the rain off my hat, trying to look non-threatening.

Nearby, a television crew was filming a reporter for a local TV station. Snippets of her words carried to my ears. "…tragedy at the racetrack…"

We inched closer to hear the reporter, but others had gotten the same idea. Even if we pushed through the crowd, I didn't want to call attention to ourselves.

Then again, Saratoga News One wasn't the only media outlet visiting the track today. Where had TJ gone? Did he know what happened? He'd be appreciative if I shot him a heads up.

As I reached for my phone, a thought struck me like a thunderbolt. Given his tendency to "embellish" stories, it seemed suspicious that I would run into TJ at the track on the day someone was murdered. How low would he stoop to get clicks on his stories?

"What are you looking for?" Cal asked.

"This is going to sound crazy." Lowering my voice, I filled Cal in on what happened while he placed our bets. "TJ wouldn't attack someone to get a good article, would he?"

Cal snorted. "TJ might, but he couldn't have gotten close enough. He's probably on the field if he didn't move inside when the rain started. Do you want to look?"

"Nah. He'll want to interview us," I said. "Should we wait for Jacob?"

"I'd say yes, but we have no idea how long he'll be. We're both wet, and you're uncomfortable in those shoes. Let me take you home. I'll check on him later."

"Tell him I'm here if he wants to talk. Losing someone you know is hard, even when they're not a friend." In my time in Shady Grove, I'd been unfortunate enough to get wrapped up in several murder cases. The shock was a lot to handle alone.

"Will do." He squeezed my hand. "Thanks. Sorry today ended so badly. I wanted to show you a nice time."

"I was having a nice time," I said.

My unspoken words hung in the air. *I was having a nice time… until the murder.*

He realized it at the same time I did. I winced at the expression crossing his face. Cal shouldn't be the sorry one. Since discovering my psychic powers, everywhere I went, death followed.

# CHAPTER FIVE

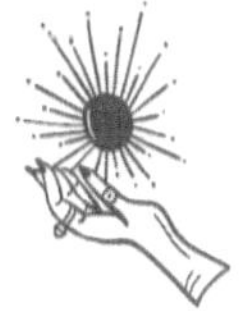

ON MONDAY MORNING, although still reeling from the events at the racetrack, I dropped in on Lucretia Kavanaugh. There was nothing I could do for Morgan, but the Kavanaugh family needed my help.

As a cover story, I had Olive make a copy of the receipt for Mrs. Kavanaugh's donation to Missing Pieces. We issued those when accepting the donation, but it was easy to fake a mix-up.

The retirement facility where Lucretia lived was new, airy, and stunning. It looked like a high-end apartment building— the kind of place where the rent was several times more than my monthly income.

Double-high glass front doors opened into a golden atrium with shimmering floors, plush seating, and a chandelier right out of *The Phantom of the Opera*. I felt underdressed in my black shorts and red T-shirt.

A concierge at the front desk stopped me from approaching the elevator banks. She was a few years older than me but wore authority like a pashmina. Maybe the skintight bun pulling her hair back helped her stand up straighter. "Can I help you?"

"Um, yeah," I said. "I'm here to visit Lucretia Kavanaugh."

"Oh! Lucy. Can I tell her who's calling?"

"My name is Aly. I'm from Missing Pieces, the antique store."

"What is the nature of your business?"

*None of yours*, I wanted to say. Instead, I went with a partial truth. "I'm here about a recent donation."

The girl sniffed before picking up her phone. She left me with the distinct impression I'd failed an unwritten exam I didn't know I was taking. After speaking with someone, she set the receiver down. "Lucy's in the gym. Please have a seat, and she'll meet you soon."

After thanking her, I took a seat. It wasn't long before the sound of my name made me look up.

A smiling woman in purple leggings and a yellow hoodie strode toward me. She wore her brown hair in a ponytail with a few strands escaping to frame her face. Despite having been in the gym, she appeared more put together than I did.

Knowing Mrs. Kavanaugh was old enough to be Olive's mother, I was surprised at how young she looked. I couldn't detect a single wrinkle on her pale white skin. Then again, Olive was younger than I'd believed. What did I know?

I rose to my feet. "Hi! My name is Aly Reynolds."

"Yes, yes, of course! I know who you are. It's delightful to meet you, dear," she said, shaking my hand. "I assume you've gone through my delivery. Thank you for indulging me."

Before we got into my reason for visiting, I shot a glance toward the front desk, where the receptionist had vanished. Good. I didn't want anyone to overhear us.

"Olive said you want me to help Tripp."

"Preston Wilcox Kavanaugh III." She smiled, lost in a memory. "His friends called him Tripp. His full name was such a mouthful, they told me, but I thought it was lovely. A strong name, full of history. Well, until his father turned into such a dud. Now I suppose I should use the nickname. One less reminder of the divorce. Anyway, I'm delighted to see you. The shipment went out so long ago, I worried you wouldn't help."

"Oh, no! We needed time to unpack the boxes. Long story, but we didn't finish until last Saturday." I hesitated. "I found a puka shell necklace that Olive said used to belong to Tripp."

"Did it give you a vision?" Her eyes brightened so much at the question, I hated to answer.

"Shh!" I glanced around to make sure no one could overhear us before lowering my voice. "How much do you know about me?"

She beamed at me. "You're a local celebrity. In the right circles, at least. I am delighted to meet you. This is more exciting than the time I spotted Mary Tyler Moore watching a Broadway show."

Her compliment warmed my heart, but did I want everyone to know me as a psychic rather than, for example, a brilliant scientist? "When you say well-known, you mean… What are people saying about me? Exactly."

"Oh, right!" She pressed her lips together and mimed locking them, then throwing away the key. "Nothing. Absolutely nothing. You're a perfectly normal girl who works at the perfectly normal antique store with perfectly normal Olive."

To punctuate her words, she tried to wink but wound up blinking as if something flew into her eye.

I snorted. "Not sure I'd go that far. But I appreciate your discretion. I just hope I can help."

"You're the first person in decades to listen. You've helped already. Let's go upstairs and chat."

I took a deep breath. "Mrs. Kavanaugh—"

"Please, my friends call me Lucy."

"Lucy, then." I smiled, hoping she'd still consider me a friend when I finished this investigation.

"Not here." She led me to an elevator, where we waited in silence.

Her desire for privacy didn't surprise me. People used to call her crazy. In a community like this, the whispered comments and wary looks would be unbearable.

We exited on the third floor. Once we'd entered her apartment, she offered me tea and pulled a bag from the cupboard. "Cookie?"

I thanked her, then tried again to tell her what I needed to say. "I'm not sure how you think I can help."

"Don't be coy with me. I've been seeking 'special assistance' with this case for years. Regular people never notice what's going on in front of them, but I'm open-minded. Strange things happen in Shady Grove, especially around you."

"Do you have any supernatural powers?"

"No, but I've been around the block a few times. Sometimes magic is the only explanation."

"Then how did you, uh, draw my attention to the necklace?"

"I didn't," she said. "Everything went into the boxes. I didn't know what, if anything, would grab your interest. What did you see? Tripp didn't do it, did he?"

She looked so hopeful; I hated to burst her bubble. "I'm sorry, I didn't see who killed Penny. The necklace showed me other scenes from the party. I'm still trying to piece it all together."

Her face fell. "Well, that's alright. Thank you for trying."

"What makes you think Tripp is innocent?"

"He loved Penny," she said. "He'd have done anything for her. I know that doesn't mean much coming from his mother, but that boy's never been able to lie to me. He was distraught after she passed and genuinely confused that anyone suspected him."

Bearing the weight of her expectations worried me. What if Tripp did it?

I took a deep breath and stuffed a cookie into my mouth, chewing for a long time before I swallowed. "I'm not a private investigator. I'm just a girl with a unique ability. Even if I identify the murderer, we might not manage to reopen the case. My visions aren't admissible in court."

She nodded. "I appreciate your honesty. Either way, knowing the truth will bring me peace. Penny's parents were dear friends of ours. Losing them hurt almost as much as the rest of it. I believe with my whole heart that Tripp is innocent, and I'll do whatever is necessary to bring the real killer to justice. By the way—what's your fee?"

Her question took me aback. "My what?"

"Your fee, of course!" She opened a drawer under the counter and pulled out a checkbook. "Naturally, I'm going to pay you for your time."

My eyes widened. Never had I expected Lucy to offer me money. I had a job. Two, actually. I worked at the antique store with Olive and went to school. Once, I'd received a reward after solving a case, but I'd never dreamed of requesting payment in advance.

Charging Lucy to help free an innocent man didn't feel right. Especially before any investigating happened. I might not find anything.

The offer was tempting, but charging Lucy didn't sit right. I shook my head. "Thank you, no. I can't take your money."

"Of course you can! I've got loads of it. More than I can ever spend. More than Tripp can spend in jail. Unless he's released, I'll never have grandchildren to spoil. In addition to the divorce settlement, I get a very generous alimony check every month." When I opened my mouth to protest further, she started writing in her checkbook. "I insist. At a minimum, I have to reimburse you for expenses. It's only fair. You'll have to drive to the prison at least once. That'll take hours. Here—it's a blank check made out to cash. If you don't fill it in, someone else might take it and clean me out."

I shook my head. Her mind was made up. But so was

mine. "My mother would disown me for charging a woman to tell her whether her son committed murder. But I'll tell you what. My friend Rusty *is* a licensed PI. He could be extremely helpful in reviewing old case files, gathering evidence, talking to witnesses, things like that. Why don't you hire Rusty, and I'll assist him?"

"Excellent plan! See that? You're already thinking outside the box." She grinned at me. "What's his number?"

I gave her the information, and we called Rusty on speakerphone. He agreed immediately. He explained his fee structure, then offered to mail Lucy a contract to review. "As soon as I receive the signed documents and the retainer, I can start work."

"Snail mail? What year is this?" Lucy asked. "Email it to me."

Rusty chuckled. "I'm happy to email everything if you have a printer. I need a signed contract for my records."

"Send it now. We've got a business center. I'll print it and send it back with your friend here."

After they discussed a few more details, Rusty thanked me for the referral and they hung up. The email arrived almost immediately, and Lucy sent it to the facility's printer.

"I'll walk you out when we're done, and we can pick it up." Lucy beamed. "I'm so excited that we'll be working together."

"Me, too!" Despite my concerns that I wouldn't find anything useful, I meant it. Lucy had a great energy, and I truly hoped Tripp hadn't killed anyone.

"Where do we start?"

"First, I'd like to hear your story." I pulled out my phone to take notes. "What can you tell me about your son?"

"Preston was such a sweet boy," she said, face softening with the memories. "He'd never hurt a fly. Wanted to be a doctor when he grew up, you know. He talked about assisting low-income patients to pay back what life had given him."

I listened to all of this with a healthy bit of skepticism.

Obviously, Tripp's mother thought he was a great person. "How did he know Penelope?"

"Penny. Everyone called her Penny. They grew up together," she said. "The Langley family lived next door. We were great friends. Maxine and I used to walk the kids side-by-side in their strollers. Penny was like a daughter to me."

Her voice cracked on the last sentence. My heart went out to her. Whether Tripp committed the murder or not, his mother had suffered. I wanted to give her closure.

"I'm so sorry," I said.

"We were devastated. I couldn't believe it. Poor, sweet Preston, arrested for murder. Then they said who they thought he'd killed." Her voice cracked, and tears filled her eyes. My heart broke for this poor woman. She hadn't just lost her son in this tragedy. "It was the worst shock of my life—twice."

"How did she die?" I asked. My brother had told me that the police never found a murder weapon. It was one of the stronger arguments for Tripp's innocence. "Is it true that she was stabbed?"

"She was, more than once," Lucy said. "A terrible crime."

That explained the blood in my vision.

"What did the coroner say?" I asked.

"Death caused by an unknown sharp object." She sighed. "I've gone through the pictures of that room a thousand times. No knife, no scissors, no broken glass... Tripp and Penny were in a bedroom at a frat house. The room contained a bed, a dresser, and a desktop computer. Nothing in the room sharper than a mechanical pencil."

"Let me guess—it didn't match the wounds?"

"Not even close." She shook her head. "They never articulated a viable theory. At trial, they argued that Tripp handed the weapon to an unknown accomplice or tossed it out the window before pretending to sleep."

"Penny was alive when Tripp passed out. What did she do after?"

"No one knows. Witnesses saw them go upstairs around midnight. The next time anyone admits seeing either of them, it was five a.m., and Penny was dead."

"Could someone have come through the window? Or been lying in wait?" Although I didn't recall anyone else in the room in my vision, I'd been focused on Tripp and Penny. They hadn't checked under the bed, opened the closets, or looked in the attached bathroom. And why would they?

Still, Penny and Tripp being accosted by someone hiding in the room before they arrived seemed less ridiculous than Tripp evaporating the murder weapon.

"Only if they brought a ladder. The room was on the second floor."

"Let me guess—no one found a weapon under the window?"

"Bingo." She shook her head. "You see why I don't buy the police's theory. Even if my son were capable of such a thing, the story defies logic."

Her skepticism made sense. Penny and Tripp were in bed together behind a closed, unlocked door. All the windows were closed. Tripp was arrested on the spot. The police thoroughly searched him and the bedroom. Presumably, when they didn't find the murder weapon, they'd checked the rest of the house.

Where did the murder weapon go? If Tripp stashed it in another room, why go back to lie beside Penny? He should have run.

Even if an accomplice took and disposed of the knife, that created bigger questions. Why hand it off to someone else? It doubled the risk of being seen and created an unnecessary witness.

On the other hand, if Tripp was so drunk he'd murdered his ex-girlfriend and passed out beside her, where was the weapon? It should have been near the bed where he would've dropped it.

In my vision, Tripp trailed behind one of his friends who

used a fencing sword to part the crowd. Could that have been the murder weapon? No. After twenty-plus years, not likely. But when I spoke with Tripp, I made a note to ask him about it.

This case called to my inner researcher because I loved solving puzzles, putting pieces together to create a whole picture. My powers also gave me a unique advantage over the local police. But I felt completely out of my depth. Was I remotely qualified to solve a decades-old murder with nothing but the goodwill of the accused guy's mother and a fractured memory? The probability of getting a useful vision was low.

Since they'd been in a frat house on my campus, I could visit the scene, but what would it tell me now? No one could have missed a clue for twenty-plus years.

"Please help," she said. "You can do things others can't."

The sadness in her eyes made me want to promise anything, but I refused to give her false hope. "Do you have an overview of the state's case? A list of the evidence, trial transcripts, anything? Was the trial televised so I can watch it?"

"Oh, no," she said. "New York doesn't allow cameras in the courtroom. There are transcripts, though. I'll ask Tripp's lawyer for copies of his records. They may need time to respond."

"Call me when you get the file. Meanwhile, I'll do some research. This could take time. I'm not a miracle worker. And again, if Tripp did it, I'm not going to lie."

She swallowed. "I wouldn't expect anything less. Thank you for your honesty. Here, take another cookie with you."

On that note, our conversation ended. While I munched on the chocolate sandwich, Lucy led me to the business center to print and sign Rusty's contract. When she gave me the contract with a new check, my eyes widened at the number of zeroes.

I promised to be in touch, then headed for my car. Our

conversation swirled in my head, but I didn't know what to believe.

Lucy had pointed out an interesting hole in the prosecution's case against Tripp, but I wasn't a lawyer. Tripp's conviction had been affirmed on appeal, which suggested there was some evidence against him.

I needed to start at the beginning.

# CHAPTER SIX

NORMALLY, the best way to gain Shady Grove intel was to ask notorious town gossip Thelma Reyes. Unfortunately, Thelma moved here after Penny's death. After leaving Lucy's home, I drove to the Willow Falls Public Library, which serviced both small towns.

They'd have newspaper articles, both bigger papers from Saratoga and the local press. Contemporary articles should be more unbiased than the thousands of Reddit threads about the case or all the opinion pieces written after the case became popular. Plus, the physical paper's articles wouldn't be stuck behind a paywall or have a bunch of ads.

The Willow Falls Public Library took up an entire block. I'd always loved the stone exterior, the pillars flanking the doorway, and the enormous windows that made the whole place feel bright and welcoming even when snow covered the ground.

In the quiet, the front door thudding shut made me wince. A large staircase in the middle of the room wound up to the second floor, which housed the children's area, study rooms, and a tax center. I didn't think they had newspapers up there.

It had been a long time since I first brought my now five-year-old nephew Kyle to story hour here, watching him toddle up the stairs. The building, at least, hadn't changed much.

A sixty-something Black woman sat behind the reference desk, peering at her screen through big round red glasses. Her gray hair was pulled back into braids that reached her waist. I waved at Consuela, the head librarian. When she noticed me, I asked if she could point me to the old periodicals.

Her face lit up. "Oh, you're in for a treat! We just redid the whole section!"

With enthusiasm she hadn't exhibited thirty seconds earlier, Consuela led me to a row of brand-new computers. A gleaming plaque on the wall welcomed me to the "Walter Sparrow Memorial Research Center."

I smiled. My friend Emma must have donated the money. Last summer, she'd received a massive inheritance from the man after whom this branch had been named, and she'd also done some research here.

Holding my breath, I typed Penny's name into the periodicals index. The list of headlines that popped up weren't obviously click-bait, but I wasn't sure how much I trusted reporters to write a balanced article.

To my surprise, on the day the trial started, I spotted Hal Crews's byline. Hal was the current editor-in-chief and owner of the *Shady Grove Sentinel*. He always struck me as fair and reasonable. Although the same could *not* be said of his son, Hal had done his best to mitigate the damage caused by his sole reporter's reckless storytelling.

My lawyer brother would tell me to skip the news reports and go straight to the public records to get the story: trial transcripts, police reports, things like that. Once Lucy got the defense file from Tripp's lawyer, Rusty and I planned to pore over it, both evidence admitted at trial and everything that wasn't. We hoped to find information not available to the general public.

However, I didn't know how much information Tripp's

former attorney kept, and I wanted the gist of the story before submitting a request for documents under the Freedom of Information Act. This case had been investigated by the Shady Grove County Sheriff's Office. The request would be reviewed by Sheriff Matthews, who disliked me immensely.

If our initial investigation swayed me toward Tripp's innocence, Rusty could do the paperwork. Rusty was living with the sheriff's favorite nephew, which might help get Sheriff Matthews to process the forms sooner. Any request from me would get "lost" in a toilet tank.

Back to the newspapers. According to Hal, an on-campus fraternity, Pi Gamma Psi, threw a big party to celebrate the end of the school year. Several recent high school graduates showed up, including Tripp, Penny, and her best friends: Tricia Gonzalez and Beth Banister.

Hold on. Banister? Our mayor was at a party the night her best friend got killed? Seeing her name caused a small twinge of sympathy. No wonder she pushed the sheriff to solve murders quickly; each case must bring brought back terrible memories. She was still evil, though.

A picture of the three friends accompanied the article. Penny stood in the middle, staring directly into the camera with a big smile and one arm wrapped around each of her friends. She'd been so vibrant, so full of life. Even in a photograph, she shone. How sad to have her future taken away.

On her left, according to the caption, was Tricia. She was shorter than Penny, with bright magenta hair. A taller girl with long, medium-brown hair and a full set of braces rounded out their trio. She'd been in my vision, too, talking to someone in the hallway when Tripp arrived at the party. She'd been an afterthought at the time, but now I clearly saw our current mayor in this girl's determined eyes and firm jaw.

I studied the image like the meaning of life hid among the pixels. If Olive could help me have a vision of the events surrounding this picture, would it help? Or would I find that someone snapped the image weeks before the party?

Shaking my head, I returned to the article. Penny had arrived at the party with her friends, but the three quickly separated. Beth told the newspaper that she'd gone to speak with another friend shortly after they'd gotten there, but the friends all noticed when Tripp approached Penny.

"He looked desperate to get her back," Beth had told Hal. "When they started dating, Tricia told Penny that boy would never get over her. I wish she'd been wrong."

According to the article, the party lasted all night. Before Penny left, they looked but didn't spot her. Eventually, they'd concluded that she left with Josh Henderson, a college freshman she'd been flirting with off and on for weeks. Hardly anyone had cell phones at the time. Tricia and Beth went home thinking they'd talk to Penny in the morning.

Hours later, shouts woke up the entire house. Another partygoer claimed he stumbled on Penny and Tripp while looking for a bathroom. Through the early dawn rays coming in the window, he'd seen Penny dead and Tripp in bed beside her.

When the guy yelled, Tripp woke up, just like in my vision. According to Hal, he hadn't said a word in his defense that morning. He didn't offer an explanation or show any other emotion. The student described Tripp as "a *Night of the Living Dead* zombie. His eyes were empty, man."

From my vision, I knew Tripp hadn't been stoned or heartless. He'd been hungover and too stunned to react. The horror of finding Penny dead beside him rendered him unable to speak.

The police arrested Tripp on the spot. At first glance, it made perfect sense. They used to date, he'd been trying to get her back, and they were together all night. Still, anyone could have entered after Tripp passed out. I kept Lucy's words about the missing murder weapon in mind.

Hal had written dozens of follow-up articles over the next several months, through the trial and Tripp's sentencing. He'd even done a short story about each stage of the appeals process. In a town too small for fast food, a teenage girl's death could feed the gossip mill for years.

At trial, Beth and Tricia testified for the prosecution about Tripp's relationship with Penny, their recent breakup (although they also didn't say why), and his later behavior. The sword guy shared a few comments to give insight into Tripp's state of mind at the party.

"He loved her, you know?" Tripp's friend Richard told the jury. "In the car, he said this was his last chance to get Penny back. I wish I'd known what he meant."

Richard must be the fencer, since he arrived at the party with Tripp. He hadn't been stricken from my list yet, although it seemed unlikely someone would stab a person multiple times with a fencing sword. But if he acquired another sharp weapon, he'd know how to use it.

The guy Penny had been flirting with, Josh, gave the most damning testimony. He'd seen Tripp and Penny stumble up the stairs together shortly after midnight. The party continued, but no one saw them again until the next morning's horrible discovery. Josh figured they'd decided to patch things up, so he'd left. According to him.

Tripp never stood a chance.

The Kavanaughs had hired a high-priced attorney from New York City to preside over their son's defense. From the beginning, Tripp maintained his innocence. He declined to speak with the police, but testified in his defense at trial. He'd sworn that he'd had a couple of drinks and didn't remember what happened after going upstairs.

If the police gave Tripp a blood alcohol test, Hal didn't mention it. I'd check the police file, but given how extensive the coverage was otherwise, I suspected they'd decided there was no point in doing the test hours after Penny died. Hal also didn't mention whether Tripp had any wounds on his body, or whether there were any signs of Penny fighting back.

Given the reporter's thoroughness and attention to detail throughout the rest of the stories, I expected that the police either hadn't gathered this evidence or never released it. Hopefully, the lawyer's file would tell me more.

At trial, Tripp's lawyer (according to Hal) skewered each witness for the prosecution, but he put on little defense other than Tripp's testimony. Tripp delivered his answers woodenly, staring at his hands and speaking so low the judge had to ask him to repeat himself. He didn't make eye contact with anyone during the entire trial.

The jury showed no sympathy for the prosecution's depiction of a spoiled rich boy who threw a "deadly tantrum" the first time someone told him no. The prosecutor used that phrase in opening and closing arguments, and it had the desired effect on the jury. They deliberated for only a few hours before returning a unanimous guilty verdict.

After leaving the courtroom, Tripp's lawyer told the papers, "Today was a miscarriage of justice. My client was in no state to stand trial. Due to his grief, his mental state had deteriorated until it was impossible to communicate effectively. The judge should have put the trial on hold while Tripp sought mental health treatment. We certainly intend to appeal."

I found other pieces in different publications, most of which contained the same general factual overview. None shed any light on who might have killed Penny other than Tripp. The new guy, maybe, after he'd seen Penny and Tripp go into a bedroom together. The defense team hadn't mentioned any alternate suspects at trial, though, so they must not have found him viable.

The high school newspaper did a two-page spread on Tripp when he was a senior. These people had money I couldn't fathom. The article told me nothing about Tripp's guilt or innocence, but it was interesting to contrast the beaming photograph of the confident senior sitting astride a million-dollar racehorse with the sunken eyes of the man who'd been arrested for murder a few short months later.

Poor Penny. Poor Lucy. Poor Tripp, if he didn't do it. And if not Tripp, who?

The police hadn't considered Josh a suspect. Personally, I wondered how upset he'd been at Penny for apparently picking Tripp. Everyone said jealousy motivated this murder. What if the jealous one hadn't been Penny's ex-boyfriend but the new flirtation?

Josh had motive and opportunity. No one found the murder weapon, but anyone in the frat house could have borrowed a knife from the kitchen, killed Penny, and then either put it back or left with it. Josh was as likely as anyone.

Lost in thought. I printed a few pages and sent some other articles to myself for review later.

Before leaving, I cleaned up my workstation and grabbed the pages off the printer. On my way out, Consuela smiled and waved.

"Thanks for your help," I said.

"Anytime! Please come back. We're happy to assist. Are you looking for anything specific?"

At this stage, I didn't want anyone to know about my interest in Penny's case. I shook my head. "Just poking around."

"Did you find what you wanted? If you need any publication we don't have, call me. I'll order it."

I thanked her and promised to be back soon.

After I settled into my car, I plugged in my phone and found several texts from Cal. Instead of texting back, I tapped the screen on the console to call him while I drove home.

"Aly! Where are you?"

His tone worried me. "What's wrong? How's Jacob?"

"Awful," Cal said. "The police invited him to the station today to ask questions. I went with him and waited outside. One of the stable hands overheard his argument with Morgan."

The words sent a shiver down my spine. "You don't mean—"

"They think Jake killed her."

# CHAPTER SEVEN

CAL'S PRONOUNCEMENT took me by surprise. How could anyone think Jacob killed Morgan? She died inside the stable while he was on the track in plain view of thousands of people. The property was crawling with workers, and the track owners must have security cameras everywhere. The police should find the culprit before dinner.

"That's impossible," I said. "Jacob was racing."

"You and I know that. The medical examiner hasn't determined the time of death yet, though. Morgan was scheduled to ride in the last race, but she didn't appear. Remember the empty slot?"

I nodded, mulling over the implication of his words. "She was already dead."

Cal said, "It's a theory. Her mount was favored to win. Jake's was expected to place. The police think he wanted that blue ribbon badly enough to kill her before lining up."

I squeezed my eyes shut and shook my head. The fact that Jacob got the blue ribbon without Morgan competing made everything worse.

"It'll be okay." With nothing to back them up, the words sounded empty even to my ears.

"Can you talk to him?" Cal asked. "He's freaking out."

"We can talk, sure, but I don't know that I can help him feel better."

"I thought maybe you could, um, offer to figure out what happened."

I hesitated. Cal's request shouldn't have surprised me. I'd helped the police with investigations in the past, and my psychic powers helped find evidence regular people couldn't. But those cases involved accessible crime scenes and people I knew. How was I going to convince strangers to share information?

On top of that, I'd just promised Lucy to help find Penny's killer. She'd given Rusty a hefty advance, and that gave her priority.

Still, the sadness in Cal's voice broke my heart. Researching a decades-old murder took time. Until we got Tripp's lawyer's file out of storage, we couldn't do much. Rusty would need to track down the witnesses, and one of us needed to contact Tripp. I didn't even know how to call someone in prison. On TV, they seemed to have lists, but how did a person get on them?

Then we needed to review the police reports and court files. It could take months to get an official response to a Freedom of Information Act request, even in tiny Shady Grove. The documents were probably sitting in Town Hall, not two blocks from Olive's store. Our courtrooms were housed inside, along with essentially every other government office, many of them staffed by the same person. Unfortunately, gathering up the information and copying it wouldn't be a priority for anyone.

Given our holding pattern, helping Jacob shouldn't take time or energy away from Tripp's case. If I could do anything to save Cal's family, I wanted to try.

Under normal circumstances, the track held races Wednesday through Sunday, with Monday and Tuesday designated as "dark days." Today was Monday. If I went to the track alone on Tuesday, I couldn't get in. I had no legitimate reason to be there.

"Can he get me into the track tomorrow, even though it's not open to the public? It'll be easier to poke around when there's less going on."

"Hold on." He relayed my question to Jacob. "Yup. No problem. Tomorrow should be business as usual."

"That was fast."

"Think about how much money the racetrack makes for the county. Money moves mountains."

"For once, I'm grateful," I said. The longer we waited before investigating, the more difficult it got.

"Thank you so much," Cal said.

"I can't make any promises."

When he spoke again, I heard a smile. "I know, but having you on Jake's side makes me feel better. You don't give yourself enough credit."

More like, I had a realistic grasp on my limitations. "We need to learn more about Morgan. Friends, enemies, rivals. What's her track record look like?"

"Can you come by my place? Jacob's sleeping in Teddy's room tonight." As a graduate student, Cal rented an apartment near the campus. His roommate had gone on a research trip for the summer, getting paid to travel to South America. We would have plenty of privacy.

"Sure. I'm on my way."

After we hung up, I turned onto the state highway and drove like I was trying to win a blue ribbon. The normally twenty minute drive took closer to fifteen.

Cal opened his apartment door with red eyes and messier hair than I'd ever seen. Something stained his wrinkled shirt, which wasn't like him. With a sigh of relief, he pulled me into a hug.

"Everything's going to be okay," I said. "Walk me through what happened."

Cal led me inside, where Jacob sat in the middle of his

couch. In his T-shirt and sweatpants, he looked much younger than his twenty-seven years. Thirty-six hours' worth of stubble covered his face.

When he looked at me, his eyes barely flickered with recognition. "You didn't have to come."

"Of course I did. I want to help."

"There's nothing you can do," he said dully. "I need a lawyer. I can't afford one."

"My brother's a lawyer. He doesn't do criminal law, but I can get you a referral."

"That I can't pay for."

"It won't be necessary," Cal said. "Aly is going to figure out who killed Morgan before the police arrest anyone."

Jacob chuckled. "Yeah, right. Thanks. I needed that."

"I'm not joking," Cal insisted, sitting on the couch next to him. "Aly's got special—"

"Inquisitive nature!" I said loudly, plopping down on the side chair. "I do a lot of research for my grad program, and it's helped me learn to analyze information objectively."

Cal shot me a look, but I shook my head. In the past twenty-four hours, Jacob had competed in his first professional horse race, won his first blue ribbon, lost a coworker, and been accused of murder. He didn't need the revelation that psychics were real. Besides, while I trusted Cal with my life, I barely knew his cousin. What if he panicked and told everyone? I couldn't investigate if every witness thought I had delusions of superpowers.

"Right. Yeah. Jake, Aly is incredibly smart. Way smarter than me," Cal said.

"Aren't most people?" Jacob asked, punching him lightly in the arm. "Seriously, I can't ask either of you to get involved."

"We're already involved," I said. "We witnessed your conversation with Morgan. That's why the police are investigating you."

Jacob's face turned even whiter. He shook his head slowly.

"You could be in danger. Stay away from this. Let the police find the truth."

"I'd love to," I said as I headed for the adjacent kitchen to make coffee. We were going to need it. "Unfortunately, Sheriff Matthews gets tunnel vision on the first suspect. We need to give him someone else to look at."

"The younger officer didn't seem so bad," he said.

"That's Doug," Cal said.

"He's fabulous, but not the one in charge. Sheriff Matthews is basically the mayor's puppet, and she'd rather he make quick arrests than waste time actually solving crimes."

Jacob's face turned from white to green.

"You need our help," Cal said.

Jacob looked like he wanted to argue further, but he shook his head. "Okay. Let's do this."

By the time I handed out coffee—cream and sugar for me and Jacob, black for Cal—Jacob relaxed.

"Thanks," he said once he gulped down the coffee. "This is perfect."

"Let's start at the beginning," I said. "Cal and I saw Morgan yesterday morning before we met up with you. She was arguing with someone. A trainer, I think."

"Tall guy," Cal said. "Lots of freckles, black hair?"

"That's Ryder," Jacob said.

"What was their relationship like?" I asked.

"Ryder just started. He met her, and everyone else, a few days ago."

"Did Morgan have problems with other coworkers?" Cal asked. "It's early in the season to be making enemies."

Jacob thought for a minute. "There are rumors. Morgan was thinking about racing for another owner. She'd get a big raise if she switched stables."

"How did Mr. Hill feel about losing her?" Cal asked. "Was he angry enough to kill her?"

"Mr. Hill's usually cool as a cucumber," Jacob said. "But

he's invested a lot in Morgan over the years. He wouldn't be happy to lose her."

None of this seemed big enough to drive someone to murder, but relationships were often more complicated beneath the surface. If a discussion turned into an argument and someone was holding a hoof pick, they might take a swing...

"I don't think this was planned in advance," I said.

"Why not?" Jacob asked.

"The murder weapon. With a planned attack, I'd expect a more obvious weapon, like a gun or knife. A hoof pick seems like the killer grabbed whatever was close at hand."

"Also, the location," Cal said. "That stable was so busy, a stranger would be spotted."

"Right. It's not a good place to execute a murder," I said.

"A stranger would be *seen*," Jacob said. "But I can't say they would be noticed. Do you know how many people work race days? We're focused on our own thing, not looking at anyone else. Unless this person drew attention, they would have been invisible in plain sight."

"Good point," Cal said.

I made a note on my phone.

"After her argument with Ryder, where did Morgan go?" Jacob asked. "You think they took the conversation away from witnesses?"

"Maybe," Cal said slowly. "Ryder did follow her."

"But we saw her a few minutes later, very much alive," I said. "Jacob, she used the stall beside you at the second race. Which she won."

"Chute."

"What? There was a gun?"

"No." He chuckled. "C-h chute, not s-h. The horses line up in chutes before the races begin. They're not stalls."

"Okay." I made another note. "Morgan won race two. Did you see her after that?"

"A bunch of us walked back to the stables together. I think Morgan was there, but I'm not positive."

"Wasn't she in another race before the one she missed?" Cal asked. "I thought I saw her later."

Jacob nodded. "She would have been scheduled in three or four. The track schedule is online."

Right. I'd been looking at it during the races.

Cal pulled out his tablet and tapped while I took notes. "When was the last time you saw or spoke to Morgan?"

"The last time we talked was when she yelled at me that morning. I figured she'd apologize once she cooled off." He shook his head. "She was next to me in the second race, so I must have seen her, but I didn't pay attention. I was completely in the zone. I wouldn't have noticed if Beyoncé said hello."

"Do you remember seeing anyone else with her?" I asked. "Morgan, I mean. Not Beyoncé."

"No. It was my first day as a real jockey! I didn't need Morgan's negativity."

"What happened after the final race? You went to the winner's circle, they took pictures, then what? Take me step by step through everything up until you found out she'd been killed."

"Why do you ask?" Cal interjected.

"The police probably asked most of these questions already." I glanced at Jacob, who nodded. "We need to nail down his story, review it from all angles. The police will analyze every detail, and we don't want them finding inconsistencies."

"I told you most of it," Jacob said. "After the race, I handed Goose to a groom for cooldown, then headed for the tack room."

"What's that?"

"It's got the horse equipment. Saddles, bridles, bits, and whatnot."

My ears perked up. "What about hoof picks?"

"Those, too."

"Is there more than one?"

"There's a ton of everything. Anyone could grab a hoof pick."

"How long were you there before someone told you Morgan died?" Cal asked.

Jacob frowned while he considered the question. "A minute or so? Not long. I walked in, put my stuff away, then someone screamed. Next thing I knew, security was herding everyone around and the police showed up."

"Do you remember who told you she'd died?" I asked.

He shook his head. "No. Everyone was talking at once."

"How many people were in the stables?" I asked.

"Most people who weren't in the last race would have watched," Jacob said. "That includes trainers, jockeys, vets, everyone. We'd survived opening weekend. They would have wanted to enjoy it."

"Then what?" Cal asked.

"The police took us into an empty stall one by one to ask questions," Jacob said. "The jockeys all said no one had seen Morgan since before the last race. The police wanted to know why we hadn't been worried."

"What did you tell them?" I asked.

He shrugged. "Morgan and I weren't friends. I don't care why she wasn't in the race. One fewer person to beat."

While I appreciated his candor, his lack of emotion made me want to tear my hair out. To the police, a murder suspect who acted so calm and collected raised suspicion. Jacob wasn't a total stranger. He knew and worked with Morgan, and hadn't been alarmed when she'd vanished.

Cal met my eyes. "It looks bad, doesn't it?"

I forced myself to relax. My anxiety would make everyone else more nervous. "Not terrible, not great. You're not skipping and whistling a jaunty tune, but the lack of sorrow over her death combined with their perceived motive is going to keep you on the suspect list until we can clear you. I wish we knew the exact time of death."

"I asked if they could compare my prints to the murder weapon, and they said no," Jacob said. "They figured the killer wore gloves."

"Doesn't everyone who works in the stable wear gloves?" I asked.

"Exactly," Jacob said.

What a bad break. I took a deep breath. "In a place like that, with those expensive racehorses, there must be security cameras about every ten feet."

"Yeah, there are," Cal said. "Just about."

Jacob said, "They glitched or something. All the footage from yesterday was gone when the police checked."

"That is highly suspicious." My mind raced, and I remembered the guards' unfriendliness. You wouldn't think someone their size could move undetected, but either of them could wander around without it seeming unusual. What if one of them killed the feed to cover his own tracks? "Could the security guards have deleted the video?"

"Probably not. It would have to be someone with a high security clearance. Unless someone hacked in."

"If it was a hacker, you're still a viable suspect," Cal said.

He rolled his eyes. "I'm no hacker, man."

"They don't know that." I pointed out.

Jacob sighed. "I'm in trouble."

"The police are looking for means, motive, and opportunity. They believe you had all three. But you could kill Morgan any day. Why now? It makes no sense to kill a jockey in the middle of the stables on opening weekend," I said. "Meet her when the track was closed. Follow her home, I don't know. Pretty much any option besides attacking in public where anyone could see you."

"Excellent point," Cal said.

"Also, why? Just because Morgan yelled him?"

"Remember what she said about Bryce? Morgan insisted someone hit Bryce's car on purpose. She thought I did it to get his spot in the race," Jacob said.

"No one believed that, did they?"

He shrugged. "I wouldn't think so, but maybe if Morgan shared her theory, someone thought I'd be a good fall guy."

"You're *in* the races," Cal said. "Why kill Morgan?"

"No idea, man," Jacob said.

"We need to talk to Bryce," I said.

"Why?" Jacob asked.

"He can tell us how he got hurt. Morgan thought his injury wasn't an accident. Did she accuse anyone else? There could be thirty other track workers with similar motives. We already know she argued with Ryder."

"Thanks, Aly," Jacob said. "I feel better already."

I forced a smile. The pressure to solve this case made my stomach hurt. Cal and Jacob were depending on me.

"Let's back up," I said. "You said Morgan was thinking about quitting?"

"She rode for Mr. Hill, like me," Jacob said. "Recently, she's been meeting with other owners. A lot of us have speculated that one of them—O'Brien—would lure her away with more money."

"How much more?" I asked.

He shrugged. "Enough that she'd have been crazy to turn him down. Hold on, do you think O'Brien killed her because she decided against the job?"

"Your boss could have killed her to keep her from leaving," Cal added.

My fingers flew across my phone's tiny keyboard. "Did you see either owner around the stable before the last race?"

"They're always around. I saw each of them several times on Sunday."

All owners had access to the stable. No one would notice any of them walking around, with or without a hoof pick.

"Can you talk to them?" Cal asked. "Feel them out a little?"

"Hold on," I said. "Jacob can't walk up to his bosses and ask if they committed murder."

The blood drained out of Jacob's face. "Oh, no. I'm not doing that."

"We're not asking you to," I assured him. "I'll go, and we'll be subtle. Can you get me into the stable tomorrow?"

"Sure. You'll have to pretend to work there."

"No problem. I'm working in the morning, but I'll text you when I'm done. Who else should we talk to?" I asked.

"Mostly, Morgan hung out with Flo. They're both from Georgia. She might know more."

"Any issues between them? Jealousy, boy trouble?"

"I dunno. Morgan had a thing with Bryce."

"Bryce, huh?" No wonder she was so upset about his car accident. It had seemed odd to verbally attack someone over an injury to a coworker. If she and Bryce were dating, that helped explain the high emotions.

"Yeah. I've seen them flirting," Jacob said. "Didn't think it was serious until she screamed at me. I texted him—"

The blood drained from Jacob's face.

Cal groaned.

"What did you say?" I asked, trying not to sound worried.

"Hold on." Jacob pulled out his phone and started scrolling. He paused, then winced.

Cal took the phone from him and read, his jaw dropping. When he recovered, he cleared his throat. "Morgan is trouble. You should get rid of her."

A groan escaped me. Why had Jacob sent that text?

Sure, the words seemed meaningless, but thoughtless comments always came back to haunt people. Didn't he watch TV?

If the police read the message, they'd be even more suspicious of Jacob. It wouldn't take long to talk to the guy Morgan had been dating, and surely Bryce would tell them about the incriminating thing their prime suspect said shortly before Morgan died.

If we didn't find more information soon, Jacob might wind up behind bars.

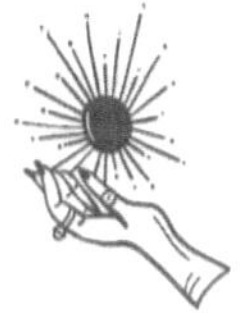

THE NEXT MORNING, finding the murderer seemed impossible. What was I thinking, agreeing to help Jacob clear his name? I didn't know anything about horses, racing, or stables. Jacob barely knew me. Why would anyone talk to me about what they'd seen or heard? Unless a police officer handed me the murder weapon to spark a vision, the likelihood of finding out anything concrete seemed slim.

Even then, I'd see what happened from the killer's perspective. Their emotions would be the ones imprinted on the weapon. That wouldn't tell me who swung the pick unless they stood in front of a mirror or Morgan said their name.

Unfortunately, I promised to help, and it was too late to back out. There wasn't anything I could do until after my shift. Meanwhile, I'd thought of something that might help with both investigations.

A question about my powers had been lingering in the back of my mind. Could I identify the subject of my visions? With Tripp's necklace, I'd guessed that I was viewing his memory from external clues: the knowledge of the object's owner combined with the K on his class ring and later, people addressing him by name. But sometimes when I had a vision, there wasn't external data. Could I learn to identify the memory holder another way?

When I entered the store, Olive stood behind the counter running the cash register. A few people browsed the aisles, so I put my stuff in the tiny staff area and relieved her. We worked side-by-side, finding items and ringing up customers.

"How are you?" Olive asked once the store emptied. "Earlier, it looked like something was bothering you."

"Not great. Someone murdered a jockey at the racetrack on Sunday."

"I heard. That's too bad." Olive clucked her tongue sympathetically. "Did Cal's cousin know them?"

"Jacob, yeah. They weren't friends, but he knew her. They argued that morning, and the police are investigating him."

"Poor guy. Are you going to help?"

"I'll try. Cal talked me into it. I'm meeting Jacob at the track later," I said. "I've been wondering, is there a way to tell whose memory I'm watching? Other than if they look in a mirror or someone says their name. Sometimes there's no one else around and it's not obvious."

"That sounds like a useful skill."

"I know! Imagine if I could pick up a murder weapon and know who wielded it. That might save Jacob. Or even Tripp, potentially. Not to mention countless others."

"Brilliant! What made you think of this?"

"When Tiffaneigh and I investigated Erica's death last spring, she asked if the killer's vision felt like one I'd had in a suspect's car. At the time, I didn't know, but I wonder. Can I do it?"

"It's an interesting idea." She thought for a minute. "I'm not sure if it's possible, but we can test it."

"How?"

"There are many items here with memories attached," she said. "Try a few."

It sounded so simple when she said it, but the sheer

volume of stuff in the store overwhelmed me. "Can't you give me something of yours to test, and I'll see if it feels like you?"

She chuckled. "I could, but if I own the item, your data is tainted. You know that. The general inventory could have belonged to anyone, so those things present more of a challenge. Regardless, I meant the stuff in the storage room. All of it came from the Kavanaugh family. See what gives you a vision and try to get a sense of the individual behind the memory."

"Excellent!" I rubbed my hands together. "Let's get started."

"Slow down. You don't get a vision from everything. It could take hours or even days to find anything else storing psychic impressions."

"Are you trying to rain on my parade?"

"Just managing expectations."

"Fine, I'm managed," I said. "What do we do first?"

"Take a deep breath. Center yourself. Do your breathing exercises. It might help if you had something with Tripp's energy to compare your vision to."

"Right. I need a control. Like the necklace!"

"Yes. I wouldn't advise wearing it while trying to have a vision from something else. When we're done, though, pull it out and compare the feelings to anything you see today."

I nodded. That made sense.

Olive kept a kettle in the back room, along with tea that enhanced magical powers. The effects were short-lived, so I rarely bothered to make a cup, but I wanted any possible boost. Learning to focus my powers could be life-changing.

While the water heated, I sat cross-legged on the floor of the storage room, breathing deeply and clearing my mind. It was harder than it sounded. My left leg fell asleep twice before the kettle started whistling. Then I had to get up, make tea, take a cup to Olive, and sit down again, now holding the teacup.

Leaning forward, I inhaled the steam. Rather than go back

to the breathing exercises, I recited the elements of the periodic table aloud. Then I sipped the near-scalding tea and set it aside before closing my eyes and starting over. Finally, a quiet confidence settled into my bones.

Olive and I had sorted and put away most of the items from this donation. I'd been helping her list items for sale online to clear out the room a bit faster. We'd meant to finish unpacking Saturday night, but my unexpected vision derailed us. The box on my right had contained Tripp's necklace. In all the excitement, I'd never unpacked the rest. Now, I pulled the flaps open.

The necklace had sat on top of some folded sweaters, which remained undisturbed. I picked up the first one and unfolded it, shaking it out. Nothing happened. Closing my eyes, I inhaled for five counts, thought of Tripp, and slid the sweater over my t-shirt.

Nothing.

Shaking my head, I took the sweater off and set it aside before moving deeper into the box. All clothes. None of them helpful. All I was doing was creating a pile of laundry before I went home.

About a third of the way through, I picked up a navy crewneck sweater and something thudded into the box. To my surprise, a knife blade gleamed against a black cotton shirt. It must have been wrapped in the sweater.

Could it be—? No, that didn't make sense. The police searched Tripp's house thoroughly after his arrest. The item they'd been looking for couldn't drop into my lap. I refused to believe Lucy had the murder weapon in her possession for almost thirty years, especially if Tripp hadn't killed Penny.

Still, I pulled on gloves before reaching for the knife like it was a snake. It was lighter than expected. While I was no expert, the weight made it feel cheap. I'd expect Tripp to have a pocketknife with a carved wooden handle and fancy steel that cost five hundred dollars an ounce or something. Then again, this wasn't your typical pocketknife. The long, curved blade looked like a hunting knife. You could slice an artery with this.

Closing my eyes, I turned the knife over in my hand and held it as if cutting meat. An image swam before my eyes.

I tried to get a sense of the person whose body I now occupied. They weren't overly tall, at least not compared to the person in front of me wearing a T-shirt and jeans. Did the energy feel male? Female? Old? Young? Tall?

No idea.

*I thrust the knife forward. To my horror, the blade disappeared inside the stranger's torso. They screamed.* I tried to drop the handle but couldn't operate the fingers in my vision.

*The victim fell to the ground with a moan. I still held the knife, although I didn't remember pulling it back. Blood gleamed on the tip.*

*Then someone laughed. The sound came from inside me.*

The vision dissolved. I screamed. The knife dropped to my feet with a dull thud.

"Olive!"

She appeared seconds later. "What's wrong? Are you okay?"

With shaky fingers, I pointed. "That knife killed someone. Not Penny. Someone else."

She took one look at the knife and burst out laughing. "You didn't think that was real, did you?"

"Of course I did! It stabbed someone!" With each word, I felt more foolish. Now that I examined it, the blade was dull. The handle *had* felt like plastic. "Why did Lucy donate a knife? You could have warned me."

"I'm sorry, Aly. I didn't know. Lucretia must have tossed it in as a novelty item for the Halloween section."

"Halloween?"

"It's a prop knife. Look." Picking up the blade, Olive pushed the tip. Instead of cutting her finger, it disappeared into the blade. When she released it, the edge shot out again, now clean. I shuddered. She repeated the motion, and once again, blood covered the blade. That was some trick. "I didn't mean to scare you. Half the kids in school had one of these. The fall before graduation, we had a *Scream* party in October."

"You had a party where everyone screamed?"

She shook her head. "*Scream*, the film. It was a huge phenomenon when it came out. We couldn't stream, you know. I saw it six times in the theaters. For the party, everyone dressed up like a character. This is a replica of the prop knife. You must've seen people playing around."

It had been ages since I'd watched that movie, but now that she mentioned it, the blade looked familiar. "Did people think it was weird that Tripp dressed up like a serial killer who tried to kill his girlfriend months before he was accused of actually killing his girlfriend?"

"At least a dozen people wore that costume, so the judge suppressed the testimony. I'll look through my old pictures if you think they would help."

I shook my head.

"It gave you a vision, though, right? That's helpful."

"I didn't get a sense of the person behind it," I said. "I was too freaked out."

"Keep trying," she said. "None of this comes easily at first."

I heaved a sigh. "I hate when you're right."

# CHAPTER NINE

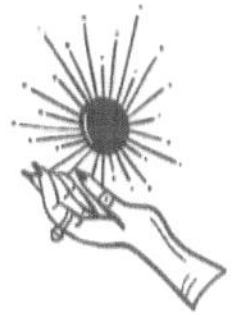

AFTER WORK, I drove through scattered showers to the racetrack. Riding clothes, it turned out, were neither cheap nor readily available in Shady Grove on short notice, so I wouldn't blend in with the workers as well as I'd hoped. My yoga pants, running shoes, and T-shirt would have to do.

When I parked my car, the sky was clear, but the horizon looked ominous. I prayed I wouldn't be stuck driving home in another downpour.

"Is the answer in the clouds?" Jacob's voice made me jump.

"I wish. Good to see you in better spirits, though."

"If I wallow, I'm useless. Need to push forward."

"That's the spirit," I said as we walked to the stables. "Any ideas where to start poking around?"

"Once we know who was here before the security cameras cut out, we can create a suspect list. Then the cops will know who to focus on."

"Great idea!"

Today, I planned to go inside the stall where Morgan died and try for a vision. The police probably blocked it off, but the fact that the stables were open made me think they'd gotten whatever evidence they wanted.

Jacob led me inside the building, moving past several horses before he nodded toward the right. "There's Wind Walker's stall. That's where it happened."

The stall contained no sign of life. Of course, the creature wouldn't tell me anything even if he stood before us—I'd never gotten a vision from a living being. Still, I hoped nothing had happened to him.

"Where's Wind Walker?"

Jacob gestured toward the far wall. "This is a crime scene, so they moved him. He's on the other side."

Excellent. I hadn't considered how the horse would react to a stranger entering his space, and now I didn't have to.

Yellow police tape criss-crossed the entrance, warning people not to enter. The bottom of the door was solid wood, but a few feet above the floor, a row of wrought iron bars around the edge separated the horses from each other and the rest of the stable. If Morgan had stood in there, caring for her horse, anyone walking by would have seen her—and her killer. The risk of getting caught in the act would be high. They must have gotten in and out in less than a minute. Why risk it?

I motioned toward a door in the far wall of the stall. "Could the killer have come in that way?"

Jacob nodded. "There are always people walking around. The trainers could be leading horses in or out at any time. But yeah, someone could come in, sneak into Wind Walker's stall, and leave."

"Wonderful. We don't even know how the killer entered." I sighed. "Are there cameras out there, too?"

"Of course, but there's no footage of anything."

Oh, fluorine. For a minute, I'd forgotten about that. The killer hadn't disabled one camera; they'd taken the entire system down.

"What's the plan?" Jacob asked. "Do you want me to stand guard while you go in?"

I nodded toward the nearest camera. A flashing red light

told me someone had fixed the system. "The security camera will capture us. Is the video monitored?"

"The guards watch everything on a big screen, but it doesn't show every feed at once. I can distract them."

"How can we distract the guards without creating a diversion that scares the horses?" I asked. "Could we talk to them about security measures? Pretend you're afraid to work here after Morgan's death. Then I'll sneak into the stall when they're not paying attention."

"It doesn't require a lot of pretending." He shuddered. "I'll ask who was here before the last race on Sunday. Reviewing the footage will take a while. When you're done examining the stall, I'll meet you in the tack room."

"Great. Where is it?"

He pointed. "That way."

The tack room sat at the end of the row, stretching across three aisles. More importantly, it was less than ten feet from an exit door. If anything went wrong, I had an escape path.

Did the killer leave this way? Curious, I pushed the door open a few inches, examining the path outside. This door led to a large grassy area and, beyond that, the parking lot. I scanned the myriad footprints—and hoofprints—until remembering Sunday's downpour. Any evidence of the killer's escape would've been washed away.

Darn it.

Sadly, I turned back to Jacob.

"Everything okay?"

"Yeah. Just wanted an option in case I need a quick exit."

He chuckled. "Each stall opens to the outside, remember? In an emergency, run out the back."

"Right. Thanks." I took a deep breath. "Okay, let's do this. Can you keep the guards talking for five minutes?"

"Piece of cake. Robert loves to explain this stuff once you get him going."

"Who's Robert?"

"One of the guards you and Cal were talking to on Sunday. Big guy, built like a linebacker."

I thought for a minute. "Does he remind you of the Hulk?"

"Less green but yeah."

Jacob led me through the rows of stalls to a room near the front. Inside, two men sat staring at a wall of screens, each showing a different image. While I watched, the monitors shifted to new views.

The Hulk looked up first. "What are you doing here?"

Jacob stepped forward. "Robert, this is my friend Aly. You met her on Sunday. Aly, this is Robert, and that's Frank."

I smiled and nodded at them. They looked at me, stone faced.

Hoping to break the ice, I gestured toward the screens. "Can you see every stall at once?"

"Those are private. Authorized personnel only," Frank said.

"She's fine," Robert said. "Any friend of Jacob's, am I right?"

"Can we help you?" Frank replied, ignoring his comment.

"I, uh, had a question," Jacob said. "On Sunday, what happened to the cameras?"

Frank groaned. "Some idiot tripped over the cord and unplugged it."

"Don't look at me!" Robert said. "Everything worked when I went to lunch."

"Do you have footage from Sunday morning?" Jacob asked.

"Why do you care?" Frank asked. "You like looking for needles in haystacks?"

Robert nudged him. "Be nice. You were just saying how boring this job is."

"Reviewing every tape is also boring," Frank said.

Jacob pulled out his wallet and removed a ten-dollar bill.

"Here. Go get yourself coffee on me. Then I can use your chair."

Frank grunted but took the money. Robert yelled after him. "Cream and sugar in mine!"

"Thanks, man." Jacob settled into Frank's vacant seat and turned toward the screens.

"Frank's right, you know," Robert said as he started typing. "It'll take forever to review everything. We've got fifty screens, and they rotate on and off."

I surveyed the panels. With so many cameras and angles, I didn't have the first clue which one covered Wind Walker's stall. The moment I walked down the aisle, I might pop up in their view.

Luckily, I'd brought my secret weapon.

Once Robert found the footage from Sunday morning, I cleared my throat. "I'm going to the restroom."

Neither of them looked up, so I ducked out, heading toward Wind Walker's stall. I forced myself to go slowly. And breathe. I needed to breathe.

# CHAPTER TEN

WITH EACH STEP, I recited the next element of the periodic table. Number 1, hydrogen. Two, helium. Three, lithium. Slow and steady, forcing myself not to rush. By the time I got to zinc, I'd reached my destination.

Taking a deep breath, I wiped my palms on my pants despite wearing gloves. The motion helped me feel better, as did reciting the next ten elements. My hands shook when I reached into my backpack and pulled out the one thing giving me an iota of faith in this scheme.

My sister-in-law, Katrina, possessed strong protective magic. Last Christmas, she'd made a pair of sunglasses spelled so people wouldn't notice me when I wore them. The spell didn't last long, and anyone who walked into me would definitely notice. Still, the guards shouldn't see me on the monitors.

Hopefully, if that happened, Jacob could convince them the screen skipped. By the time everything cycled back around, they'd have to conclude I'd moved out of range. It made more sense than a person vanishing into thin air, so they should glom onto the ordinary explanation. People usually did.

When the coast was clear, I slid the sunglasses on. Then I

gripped the handle to open Wind Walker's stall. No one called out, so I opened the door enough to slip under the police tape. The whole time I listened for signs that I'd been detected. The silence reassured me. Jacob had done his job.

After shutting the door, I lowered myself below the open bars and surveyed the area. The stall was smaller than expected. Poor horse didn't get much room to move. Putting Morgan and her killer in here with a Thoroughbred would be tight.

Other than a reddish-brown stain on the packed clay floor, the stall was empty. I assumed the police had removed any sawdust or hay, taking it as evidence. They must have tested this blood sample, but they hadn't cleaned up the stuff left behind.

Bending down, I took a deep breath, focusing on my power. In my mind's eye, I pictured Morgan, breathed deeply, and asked the stain to show me what happened here. Then I ran my fingers along the floor.

*"What are you doing here?" Morgan's voice asked.*

*Terror. Hooves pounding. A whinny, then another. Wind Walker was frantic. He thrashed as if trying to escape.*

*If anyone responded to Morgan's question, I couldn't hear them over the poor creature's distress. A heartbeat later, Morgan crumpled to the floor. The horse reared and neighed again. Something metal thunked to the ground beside Morgan—the hoof pick, presumably. Then a stall door banged shut. Front or back, I couldn't see. The sound reverberated.*

That was it. The murder happened fast, and Wind Walker's position completely blocked my view. With the palpable fear, I couldn't identify other emotions, much less who felt them. From this vision, I'd gleaned exactly one piece of information: Morgan knew her attacker.

Considering the person who killed her needed access to the private area where Morgan worked, that came as no surprise. The track employed a lot of people. While most of them worked in other areas, we still had at least fifty people who could've done it.

My phone buzzed in my pocket, informing me that my time was up. I turned off the timer, then peeked through the bars. No one was there. Quickly, I slipped out of the stall, shut the door behind me, and darted toward the tack room.

The rich scent of leather hit me in the face. I inhaled deeply, savoring it. The strength of the odor surprised me until I noticed the volume of equipment.

Dozens of saddles rested on short posts set in the wall, each with a bridle hanging from a hook above it. A number identified each set of items. I presumed they corresponded to stall numbers but hadn't paid attention while walking the aisles.

Could Wind Walker's tack tell me anything? He'd been wearing it when Morgan died. Typically, to get a vision from something, I needed to use it in the intended manner. The most obvious way to "use" a saddle and bridle meant putting them on a horse and riding it. Unfortunately, it wouldn't help Jacob if I got arrested for stealing a multi-million-dollar racehorse. What would that prove, anyway? Morgan died between races. Wind Walker never ran on Sunday.

It might be moot, anyway, without a way to find his tack. I didn't have time for a thousand visions. I needed to find the right stuff before galloping off on a wild goose chase.

As I debated my next step, I realized Jacob couldn't find me while wearing the sunglasses. The room was empty, so I slid them off and stored them in my bag.

A woman's voice made me jump. "Who are you? Where did you come from?"

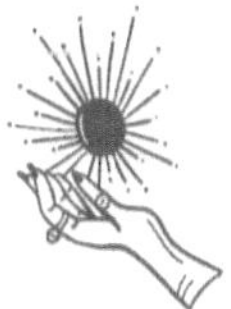



PANIC SEIZED me at the realization that a total stranger saw me materialize out of thin air. My heart pounded as my fight-or-flight reflex urged me to run. Fleeing would only make things worse, though. I'd have to bluff.

Behind me, a girl around my age sat in the corner, huddled between a barrel and the wall. The shadows concealed her almost entirely. No wonder I hadn't seen her.

"Are you okay?" I asked, ignoring her question.

She lifted her head, showing brilliant purple eyes that had to be contacts. The redness and mascara streaks told me she'd been crying for a while. Her short, dark hair was a mess. "You —you just appeared."

Although I felt terrible taking advantage of her distress, I couldn't say I walked in wearing invisibility sunglasses. The magic police had warned me about stuff like this. They could wipe her memory if necessary, but they'd give me a very stern lecture. Their leader, Lilia, might even swipe my sunglasses.

"I've been here a couple of minutes," I lied. "I just bent down to tie my shoe. You must not have noticed until I stood up."

She regarded me dubiously before apparently deciding to accept my explanation. People loved to avoid contemplating that the supernatural might be, well, natural. "Who are you? What are you doing back here? This is a private area."

"I'm Aly," I said. "My friend works here. I got a VIP pass."

"The VIP pass doesn't include wandering around the tack room unsupervised."

Okay, this wasn't going well. "Sorry, I didn't know. I just wanted a behind-the-scenes look. Do you know what these numbers mean?"

"Yes." She didn't elaborate.

This was pointless. Jacob would know how to find Wind Walker's tack. "Sorry to bother you."

I was almost out the door before she spoke again. "Wait. It's not your fault I'm upset. My best friend was killed on Sunday."

She knew Morgan? I turned back. "I'm sorry for your loss. My boyfriend and I were here on Sunday. We couldn't believe it."

She struggled to her feet, towering over me. She wore riding clothes, although nothing as fancy as the finery Jacob and Morgan wore on Sunday. "I'm Florence."

The name rang a bell, but she didn't need to know Jacob had mentioned her. "Are you a jockey?"

"Me? No way," she said. "I'm an assistant vet, still going to school. I love being around horses but can't ride to save my life."

"Me neither," I confessed. "How long did you know Morgan?"

"Since we were five years old. I can't believe she's gone. We had breakfast together on Sunday. We share a dorm during the season. I don't understand how this happened. It feels like an alien is controlling my body. My best friend dies, and two days later I'm at work like everything is fine."

Losing a friend was difficult enough. Working in the place where they died must be excruciating. My heart went out to her. "Can you take a few days off? Is her family doing a service?"

She hiccuped and shook her head. "The funeral is being held in Georgia, so I can't go. I could take a sick day, but being alone in our room makes me feel worse. I'll be okay."

"I met Morgan on Sunday morning," I said. "She seemed so full of life."

Florence sniffled. "I can't believe I wasn't here! Maybe I could have saved her."

"Do vets get the weekends off?" I asked.

Florence cackled. "I wish. No, I called out. Car trouble."

Hold on. Bryce was injured in a collision on Saturday, and Florence's car needed repairs on Sunday? I hadn't put much faith in Morgan's belief that Bryce's injury wasn't an accident, but now I wondered if I'd dismissed her concern too easily. It seemed far-fetched but too big a coincidence to ignore.

"Couldn't you ride to work with Morgan?"

Unless she'd been trying to hide that her car needed repairs. Why else would she skip work on the second day of track season?

She shook her head. "I was planning to drive up to Montreal on my day off tomorrow. Now the trip doesn't seem important."

"You didn't take your car to that place in Saratoga, did you?" I shook my head in an exaggerated show. "They charged me an arm and a leg for an oil change a few months ago."

"No, the shop's in Shady Grove," Florence said. "I don't remember what it's called."

To my knowledge, we had exactly one auto repair shop in Shady Grove, located not far from Main Street. Nothing was far from Main Street. "Are you talking about Kind of a Big Wheel? Mike's great. Straightforward with totally reasonable prices."

"I don't remember his name," Florence said. She looked me up and down. "Anyway, you can't be here by yourself."

"Yeah, okay. I want to place a bet before the races start, anyway. Show my support and all that."

"There aren't any races today. The track is closed to the public."

"Oh, right. Then I'll come back tomorrow."

"I wouldn't do that if I were you," she said. "Gambling is a nasty habit."

My gut reaction was to blow her off, but her tone stopped me. "Do you have a gambling problem?"

"Of course not. Track employees aren't allowed to gamble. Even if—" She clapped one hand over her mouth, and her eyes widened.

Before I could ask her to finish her sentence, she ran out the door.

# CHAPTER TWELVE

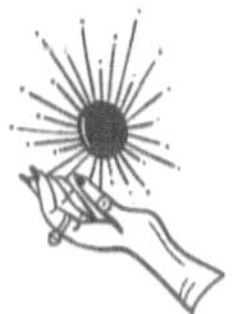

FOR A LONG MOMENT, I stared at the empty space where Florence had been. Part of me longed to go after her, make her tell me more about gambling racetrack employees. It might be nothing, but my gut said to keep an eye on her.

I turned back to the walls, looking for some kind of key or clipboard with a handy list of information. There had to be a way to figure out which tack belonged to each horse.

"What are you looking for?" Jacob asked from behind me.

I swallowed my sigh of disappointment. I'd hoped to induce a vision before Jacob got back. He could help me find the right tack, but then he needed to go.

"I wanted to see what a hoof pick looks like," I said, thinking quickly. It was sort of true. It might be easier to solve the case if I knew what the murder weapon was. "Did you find anything on the security footage?"

"Only that a ton of people work here, which I knew," Jacob said. "Frank was right. Sorting through all the footage is a fool's mission."

"The police will scour whatever they got on Sunday," I said. "Hopefully they'll find something."

"As long as I don't have to keep looking. Anyway, the

hoof picks are in here." He led me to a stack of drawers built into the wall and opened the one about chest-high.

All kinds of metal components were carefully arranged in compartments. Bits, hooks, clamps? I didn't know what most of this did. Jacob only needed a second to find what he wanted. He pulled out a small, curved metal hook and held it out to me, handle first. It looked like something the dentist would use to scrape teeth. I took the pick, weighing it in my hand. It had a decent heft to it, more than I'd expect. If swung by the right person, even getting hit with the blunt end would hurt. But the tip was long and pointed.

Curious, I touched it with the tip of my finger. Ow!

It sliced neatly into the skin. Wincing, I pulled back and offered the tool to Jacob.

"Sorry, I should have warned you not to touch it," he said. "Let me find you a bandage."

While he located a first aid kit and wrapped my finger, I told him about the bloodstain in Wind Walker's stall. I ignored everything else. People reacted weirdly to hearing about my psychic powers. Since my vision hadn't yielded useful information, there was no point in mentioning it.

Jacob's face fell. "It was a dead end?"

"Unless Wind Walker decides to tell us how the stain got there, yeah."

He heaved a sigh. "Well, it was worth a shot. What now?"

It only took a moment to recap my conversation with Florence. "I need to talk to her again."

"Do you think she had something to do with this?"

"I don't know," I said. "Her grief seemed genuine, but she volunteered that she hadn't been here on Sunday too quickly. I didn't ask. Between that and the timing of her car trouble, she's on my suspect list. What do you know about her?"

"Like I said the other day, she and Morgan were friends."

"You should talk to her," I said. "She doesn't know me. But you know her, you knew Morgan, and you can ferret out tension in their relationship."

He nodded. "Sure. Do you mind waiting here? She'll tell me more if I'm alone."

Did I mind the opportunity to poke around the tack room, look for the equipment that Morgan planned to put on Wind Walker before she died, and induce a vision? Nope.

"I'll be fine," I said, trying to mask my excitement. "Hey, before you go—how do you know which stuff goes to which horse? I assume it's not interchangeable."

He chuckled. "No, definitely not. The numbers match the stalls. Are you looking for anyone specific?"

"I wanted to see Wind Walker's tack."

"Why?"

An excellent question. I couldn't tell him I hoped to induce a vision of Morgan during one of the races that might help. "I thought there might be some clue. Blood or something."

"Good thinking. I'll find Wind Walker and text you the number before talking to Flo."

"Perfect, thanks."

My phone beeped with a message a moment after he left. I beelined for the wall of saddles and found myself staring at Wind Walker's empty spots.

Duh. Morgan had been preparing for her ride with Wind Walker when she was killed. The police probably took the tack to test it for fingerprints or DNA.

How else could I find out what happened? Morgan spent all day in the stable or on the track. Did she shove another horse out of the way moving into the home stretch? Maybe if I got inside her head, something would jump out.

It was a long shot, but I didn't have any better ideas. I needed to see what the equipment from her other horses could tell me.

In her first race of the day, Morgan rode Maverick. I'd have to check his stall number myself. With a silent prayer, I slid my sunglasses back on and hurried down the rows.

Thankfully, I made it there and back without incident.

When I re-entered the tack room, I found Maverick's saddle and bridle a few feet from the door, gleaming as if they'd recently been polished.

The posts holding the saddles stood a couple of feet apart, about three feet off the floor. With effort, I could squeeze between Maverick's saddle and the one beside it, but there was no room to sit. I'd smack my head on the bridle, but if I held it, then I couldn't use the saddle. Maybe if I pretended to be mounting a horse, I'd see something? I put one foot in the stirrup and gripped the front and back of the saddle. Reaching for my powers, I tugged gently.

The saddle slid off its perch, sending me toppling into the rack beside it. The weight of it surprised me, and I dropped it, narrowly missing my toe.

Oof. I put it back and dusted it off, glad no one had witnessed my fall. I picked up the bridle, then realized I didn't know what to do. Even if a horse stood in front of me, that wouldn't help. Which part went on top? The long straps were presumably reins, but the rest could have gone almost anywhere.

Feeling ridiculous, I stuck my face in the straps. The bit touched my nose, but I couldn't bring myself to put it between my teeth. Instead, I clutched the reins in my fists, shaking them as if urging a horse to go faster. Closing my eyes, I reached for my powers.

*A dappled gray horse carried me through the air. From this vantage point, I could only see a mane and the finish line zooming toward me, closer with each heartbeat. A group of horses entered the home stretch practically as one. I stood in my stirrups, urging my mount toward the finish line. Victory was within reach. My gaze flickered to Jacob, slightly ahead of me. If he concentrated much harder, his horse would soar into orbit.*

*The red-clad rider to my left wore the same look of determination. So did the orange-wearing jockey in my line of sight. I leaned forward, practically willing my horse to inch past the others. Even* knowing Morgan was about to win, the suspense made me squeeze the reins like I could urge her horse faster.

*The finish line loomed ahead. Maverick surged forward, as if he wanted the win as badly as I did. Under my breath, I whispered, "Go, go, go!"*

*Maverick thundered through the white ribbon. I cheered and screamed, pumping one fist in the air. My horse slowed. A huge sigh of relief escaped me.*

*Under my breath, I muttered, "It's over."*

Once again, I found myself standing in the tack room, still holding the bridle. Quickly, I replaced it before anyone could walk in and ask me what on earth I was doing. Morgan's words echoed in my head.

*It's over.*

# CHAPTER THIRTEEN

WHEN I LEFT the tack room, I'd intended to look for Jacob, but a familiar-looking figure drew my attention. Someone was leading a horse out to the exercise ring. Although his back was to me and a hat covered his hair, the guy's height and the breadth of his shoulders made me think it might be Ryder, the trainer who argued with Morgan on Sunday morning.

I pushed through the door and approached the ring. Ryder—it was definitely him—stood in the middle, talking to a horse while walking him around the circle on a long lead. When he turned to face me, I noticed an angry red scratch down the left side of his face. It hadn't been there on Sunday morning.

A broad smile crossed his face. "Hello, there. What is a girl like you doing in a place like this?"

It took effort not to wince at the cheesy line, but Ryder's flirtatious nature might work to my benefit.

"My friend is a jockey here. I saw you talking to one of the other jockeys on Sunday morning—"

"You saw us?" He shifted uneasily, and his hands tightened on the lead. The horse slowed.

"I was part of the tour group." No need to say more.

"Oh, right." His face clouded. "Sorry to subject you to that. Morgan and I were having a friendly conversation, and things got a bit intense."

"Would you say you normally got along?"

"Normally? I just met Morgan last week." He patted his horse before turning back to me. "Why do you ask?"

"Not long after I saw the two of you talking on my stable tour, Morgan yelled at my friend for no reason. If your conversation upset her, it would explain a lot."

Ryder shrugged. "It was nothing. I asked her out, she said no."

"That made her kick a bucket across the stable?"

"Uh, no. It's possible that after she declined, I said some stuff about her boyfriend. I'm not proud."

"What kind of things?"

He rubbed the back of his neck, avoiding my gaze. "The usual. Not a real man, blah, blah. I know it was a jerk move."

"After you said hello to our tour group, why did you follow her?"

"I didn't. Not on purpose. I guess we used the same door, but I went to the training ring. Morgan wasn't there. Next thing I knew, someone killed her." He sighed.

Ryder wasn't disclosing the whole truth. Morgan had been too angry for a couple of insults about Bryce. Something told me he'd kept pushing, refused to take no for an answer. Getting rejected was the kind of thing that could lead to hitting someone in the heat of passion. Ryder was a big guy. If he swung a hoof pick, he'd have a lot of force behind it.

"You didn't follow Morgan and try to convince her to change her mind?"

"Why? Women are a dime a dozen. I'm not going to waste my time chasing someone who doesn't like me."

A valid point, although not the perspective I'd expected from someone who'd admitted to insulting Bryce because Morgan didn't want to date him.

Rather than respond, I changed the subject, letting my

eyes linger over the angry red mark on Ryder's cheek. "That scratch looks painful! Are you okay?"

"Oh, this?" He touched it, then flinched. "It's not so bad."

"What happened?"

"None of your business." His eyes narrowed. "Excuse me, I have to work."

Ryder turned his back on me and urged the horse forward. He was hiding something. Guessing that Morgan caused the scratch had been a shot in the dark, but whatever happened, Ryder didn't want to talk about it.

If he and Morgan argued after she rejected him, her response to seeing him enter Wind Walker's stall might be, "What are you doing here?"

After thanking Ryder for his time, I went back in to find Jacob talking to Florence near a horse's stall.

"Sorry about earlier," she said. "Jacob told me you're okay. Talking about Morgan upsets me. I hate that I missed my last chance to—Anyway, sorry."

"I understand." I reached out tentatively. The horse—See Dick Run—sniffed my hand, so I stroked his nose softly. "Listen, you were saying something about track workers betting on the races?"

Her face went white. "No. I never said that."

"We're forbidden from betting," Jacob said.

Sure, but Florence knew at least one track employee gambled, anyway. I needed her to tell me who. Her denial told me not to push the issue in front of Jacob. She might worry that he'd turn the gambler over to their bosses.

Maybe Morgan placed bets on one of her races. The betting windows opened early. If Ryder had seen her, that might explain their argument. Was that why she got killed?

"It's grounds for immediate termination," Florence said. "No one would take that risk for a few bucks."

"Did you talk to Morgan before she was killed? Any DMs after she left for work?" Knowing when Morgan sent her last text would narrow the window we needed to investigate.

"She left before I woke up," Florence said. "And like I mentioned earlier, I was gone all day."

Again, she made a point of distancing herself from the crime scene. Why? Florence could have driven to the mechanic, established an alibi, and returned secretly. She knew the stable; no one would think twice about seeing her. They wouldn't notice at all, like Jacob said. Did she know how to break the security system?

Parts of this hypothesis fit, but Florence didn't have an obvious motive. Why would she kill her best friend? I wanted to know if the damage to Florence's car matched the collision, but I might be tilting at windmills.

"Hey, Jacob, didn't you want to talk to Mr. Hill before you left? We should find him before it gets too late."

"Oh, yeah, right. I haven't seen him around."

"He left," Florence said.

"Do you know where he went?" I asked.

"You ask the weirdest questions. No, the rich guy who owns half this stable doesn't tell me where he's going when he leaves. And the governor never gives me her daily itinerary. Can you believe it?"

"Aly doesn't mean any harm," Jacob said. "She's going to help me solve—"

I began coughing violently, dragging Jacob down the hall and away. Florence turned her attention back to the horse.

"We don't want everyone to know we're investigating!" I hissed once we turned a corner. "There are people all over this place. What if the killer overhears you?"

Jacob flushed. "Sorry. I didn't think about that."

I shook my head. "It's fine, but be careful. People talk. We need to keep a low profile."

Until we got more evidence, everyone was a suspect. Even if she didn't kill Morgan, Florence probably knew the person who did. She could casually mention our investigation to the wrong person without knowing it.

"I guess I shouldn't have told Robert, either," Jacob said, interrupting my pity party.

A groan escaped me. What had I gotten myself into?

# CHAPTER FOURTEEN

THE SKIES CLEARED BRIEFLY, so I asked Jacob if we could visit Bryce before the storm clouds rolled back in. If we waited for nice weather, we could be sleeping at the stable.

I'd expected to find Bryce in the hospital. Morgan made it sound like he'd been horrifically injured. Instead, Jacob directed me to drive to the far side of the track, behind the stables. A two-story white building was tucked away beside a large parking lot. The drive took less than two minutes. I was about to suggest that we could have walked when the skies opened again. Scratch that.

Squinting, I peered through the sheets of rain as I parked. "Bryce lives at the track?"

"It's a dorm," Jacob said. "A bunch of us live here, in single or double units. Bryce's apartment is upstairs. Morgan and Flo live down on one."

Now that he mentioned it, I remembered. "That's right. We saw one on our tour. Do you live here, too?"

"Nah. I'm staying with my mom."

Lightning sliced through the air. I gazed at the sky, willing the rain to stop. Now that would be a cool superpower.

"Do you want to wait?" he asked. "It should pass soon."

"No. Just wishing I had an umbrella."

"I can go in alone," he offered.

"Then I'm not helping." With a sigh, I checked the back seat for a makeshift umbrella. A-ha! I'd forgotten to return the outfit Olive loaned me to wear to the track. I'd carefully folded the dress, shoes, and jacket into my backpack, but the hat didn't fit. It waited on the back seat, pink feather proudly standing at attention. I lunged for it.

"This should work. I don't have anything for you, though, except a paper grocery bag." They lived in my car in preparation for unexpected grocery runs, both because my brother always had a ton and the reusable ones cost money.

"Better than nothing." Jacob took the bag and held it over his head before grasping the handle. "Ready? I'll race you to the door."

Before I could respond, he was gone. I yanked the hat on and followed, narrowly missing stepping in a puddle forming at the curb.

We were halfway up the path when the door burst open. A tall, thin man in a pin-striped suit brushed past me, hunched under a huge black umbrella. As he passed, his elbow clipped my shoulder. The guy didn't even slow down.

"Ow!" I yelled after him, looking for a reaction.

Nothing. What a jerk.

Then Jacob stopped and turned. The bag he was holding over his head slipped, drenching him. "Mr. Hill?"

The storm swallowed his words. If the other man heard, he gave no indication. He didn't even slow down.

Hunched over against the wind, we again raced for the stoop. When we got under the overhang, I stopped to shake the water off my hat. "Mr. Hill? Was that your boss?"

"Maybe," Jacob said. "Don't know why he's here. He's not the type to make goodwill visits to injured employees."

"Weird that he wouldn't say hi." I glanced toward the sky. "Or not."

"I could be wrong. That umbrella covered his face, and I was concentrating on not getting soaked."

"Did you see Mr. Hill's car in the lot?"

He shook his head. "I wasn't looking."

The giant double doors at the front of the building were locked, but a keypad mounted on the wall contained a giant speaker. Jacob reached past me, punching in numbers to call Bryce.

"Hello?"

"Hey, man, it's Jacob. I've got a friend with me. We want to see how you are."

The speaker crackled. "Come on up. It's open."

A buzzer sounded, and the door unlocked.

Jacob ushered me inside. "After you. Elevator is on the left."

When we reached the second floor, Jacob led the way down the hall. I followed, taking in the clean white walls and dark carpet. He banged on the door to the fourth apartment on the right. Without waiting for a reply, he pushed it open and stuck his head inside.

"Bryce? You here?"

"I'm here. Sorry, I can't get up."

Jacob pushed the door open and moved into the sparse room. Nothing decorated the white stone walls, and the floor's threadbare beige carpet reminded me of my own recently vacated dorm room. Against the far wall was a bed covered in dark blue sheets sitting atop drawers built into the bed frame. A guy who must be Bryce sat against a stack of pillows, legs extended in front of him. A cast encased his left leg, and his arm was in a sling. An empty wheelchair sat beside the bed.

A bandage covered greasy hair that might have been light brown. The poor guy also sported two black eyes and a split lip.

Jacob stopped dead upon seeing his friend's condition. "Are you okay?"

"Fine, fine! Never been better." He beckoned us to come in, so we stepped further into the room, shutting the door behind us.

"I'm Aly," I said. "A friend of Jacob's."

"I didn't know Jacob was seeing anyone."

Jacob glanced at me, and I shook my head. Bryce didn't need to know we were investigating Morgan's death.

"Are you okay?" I said instead.

Jacob picked up on my change of subject. "You're lucky to be alive, man."

"Oh this?" He waved one hand. "It's just a scratch. I'll be riding again soon."

"Right." Jacob forced a smile.

"Is someone taking care of you?" I asked. "How do you get food and stuff?"

"My girlfriend was supposed—" He closed his eyes, and pain flashed across his face. "The other jockeys are helping."

I nudged Jacob with my elbow. Our eyes met, and I gestured toward Bryce as subtly as I could. Once I mouthed an apology, he seemed to understand.

"I'm sorry about Morgan," Jacob said.

"Thanks." Bryce's voice cracked. "I'd give anything to go back and save her."

"How long were you dating?" I asked gently.

"About six months. She was something special."

"Did you see her after your accident on Saturday?"

"She wanted to visit the hospital, but I refused. This is bad enough." He gestured toward his legs. "I said I'd see her after work Sunday."

"Does that mean you didn't see her over the weekend?" Jacob asked.

"Yeah. She was supposed to pick up dinner and head over after her last race." His voice cracked. "Maybe if I'd been there with her, she'd still be alive."

"Don't beat yourself up," I said. "You couldn't have

known. Even if you'd been at the track, you might not have saved her."

"My brain knows that, but my heart doesn't understand."

"Can you think of anyone who wanted to hurt Morgan?" I asked. "Someone took a risk killing her in broad daylight when anyone could have walked by. Especially with security cameras everywhere."

Bryce shook his head. "No way. It doesn't make sense."

"She didn't have any enemies?"

"Of course not. What regular person has 'enemies'? This isn't TV." Bryce looked at Jacob. "What's up with Nancy Drew here?"

"Aly really likes true crime," he said. "Don't mind her. What do you think happened to Morgan?"

"I wish I knew." He sighed. "Sorry, I'm no help."

Quickly, I changed the subject. "Did we pass Mr. Hill on our way in?"

"Oh, yeah! Weird, huh? He said he wanted to make sure I was okay," Bryce said. "But he was here for three minutes. I guess the cast assured him that I'm not faking?"

My eyes went to his leg. "Some people get uncomfortable in hospital-like settings."

"Whatever," Bryce said. "I asked about paid time off. He got twitchy and left."

Jacob and I exchanged a look. Acting weird wasn't proof of murder, but Bryce's question seemed reasonable under the circumstances. Any employer should anticipate being asked about benefits when someone needed extended leave.

"Does he normally act like that?" I asked.

"Like he likes money?" Bryce said. "Yup."

"Mr. Hill is always concerned with the bottom line," Jacob said to me. "That's why Morgan was thinking about leaving —she wanted higher pay."

"Thinking about?" Bryce laughed. "Oh, no. She was gone. She'd been promised a huge signing bonus. O'Brien planned to give her the contract on Monday. Morgan was so excited, she almost convinced me to leave with her. Now… well, now, I'm not going anywhere. Except maybe to sleep. These painkillers are pretty strong."

"How did Mr. Hill respond to losing her to a competitor?" I asked.

"We didn't talk about it. There's no point now," Bryce said. "Hold on. You don't think he killed her, do you?"

"No, not at all," I said to Bryce, although I wondered. If Mr. Hill murdered Morgan, we didn't want him to know about our suspicions until we had proof. Besides, if he got upset that Morgan was leaving his stable, killing her didn't resolve that concern. Unless… had Mr. Hill hit Bryce's car as a warning?

"We should talk to Mr. Hill," Jacob said to me.

Ignoring him, I asked Bryce, "What happened on Saturday night?"

"It was so fast. This car burst out of nowhere, gunned it hard, slammed into me, then drove away. My car spun around like a top. I don't know if I blacked out or what, but I opened my eyes and there was this massive fried chicken sign above me. I thought I'd gone to fast-food heaven until I realized it was an actual restaurant."

Even allowing for the painkiller-fueled embellishments, something seemed off. What Bryce described sounded more like a targeted attack than an actual accident. The other driver didn't slow, didn't swerve, didn't honk, and didn't stop. What if Morgan was right?

"Can you think of any reason someone would want to hurt you?"

"Me? Nah! I'm a fun guy. Like a mushroom!" He grinned. "Get it? I'm a fungi!"

"How are those painkillers?" Jacob asked.

"Awesome! It took a minute, but now the pain is gone. I could run a marathon."

This conversation was quickly deteriorating. Soon Bryce

wouldn't be capable of speech at all. Still not willing to give up, I asked, "Did you recognize the car that hit you?"

"It had these bright white lights on the front, you know? And wheels. Yeah, it totally had wheels."

I sighed. "Thanks. That's helpful."

Jacob put a hand on my arm. "Aly, we should go."

"Jacob, you still work for Mr. Hill. You said he's like a father to you. If he's dangerous, you need to know."

Bryce said, "Playing detective seems fun. Can I go undercover?"

"Great idea," Jacob said, patting his arm. "We'll call when we need you."

"Sorry, Bryce, I know you need to rest," I said. "Just one more question. How well do you know Florence?"

"Flo? She's a cool chick. At least until Morgan and I started hanging out. Morgan said Flo didn't like her dating another jockey. I…. think she was jeal…ous." His eyelids drooped.

"How much did she not like you dating her friend?" Minor details were starting to gain significance. First Florence's car needed to be repaired the day after the accident, and now she didn't like Bryce dating her best friend. Maybe I'd dismissed her too quickly.

His eyes popped open. "She stopped talking to me. Her loss, I'm great."

"It sounds like she wanted to protect her friend," Jacob said.

How badly? Enough to break Bryce's legs? I didn't see how that would lead to Morgan's death, though. Unless Morgan found out that Florence had hit Bryce's car and threatened to call the police. That kind of argument could lead to a physical altercation.

"Would Florence have hurt you to keep you from beating Morgan in a race?" I asked.

"No way," Bryce said. "Morgan would've been big mad. She didn't need Flo's help. She rocked."

Closing my eyes, I recalled the images from my vision, with Maverick's thundering hooves and Morgan's excitement. "She flew down the track like her horse had wings."

"Too bad she couldn't fly away before someone killed her," Bryce said, closing his eyes. I waited for them to reopen, but his breathing slowed. The painkillers had taken over.

"Thanks for talking to us," I said, although he couldn't hear me anymore. "I hope you're back in the saddle soon."

# CHAPTER FIFTEEN

SHAKING MY HEAD, I followed Jacob down the stairs. None of this made sense. There was no reason for Mr. Hill to ignore us in the parking lot. Even in the pouring rain, it only took a second to nod a greeting. Why had he come? Bryce and Jacob were both surprised to see their boss, but maybe Mr. Hill had an ulterior motive.

Then there was Florence. Bryce said she couldn't stand him. Did she despise him enough to hit his car? She had easy access to hoof picks, and no one would question a vet walking the aisles. Florence and Morgan could have been arguing about Bryce, and Florence hit her in the heat of the moment. Sure, Florence said she went to the mechanic, but I only had her word.

The pieces didn't fit. For one thing, there was no reason to think she knew how to disable the security cameras. Of course, anyone could pull a power cord, if they knew where to find the right one.

When we reached the ground floor, something tugged at my memory. I pulled Jacob to a halt. "Did you say Florence and Morgan live here, too?"

"Yeah." He gestured down the hall. "Last door on the left.

Why? Flo's probably still at the stables, if you want to ask her more questions."

"That's what I'm hoping."

Jacob tilted his head at me. "What are you saying?"

"Oh, um, nothing. Go wait outside. I'll be there soon."

"Why?"

"Plausible deniability." If he didn't know what I was planning, he couldn't accidentally give me away. Or get fired for aiding and abetting. "Text me if you see anyone coming, okay?"

Jacob looked like he wanted to ask more questions, but he went outside and sat on the stoop.

I hurried to the door he'd indicated. When Rusty became a PI, he'd taught me how to pick locks. Bought me a set of picks and everything. They'd come in handy more than once, and now I carried them everywhere.

Thankfully, the hallway was deserted. Pulling the picks out of my pocket, I dropped to my knees and examined the lock. Whoever owned this building certainly wasn't spending much on security. This lock looked flimsy enough to be opened with a credit card. Either the jockeys trusted each other, or none of them owned much worth stealing.

After a couple of seconds, the mechanism popped open. I hurried inside, closing the door silently behind me.

The room resembled Bryce's, except there were two of everything: nightstands, beds, dressers, each with a toiletry bag on top. A coffeemaker stood on one. Both beds were neatly made. Someone had hung horse racing posters on the right-hand wall, so I guessed that was Morgan's side.

What was I looking for? Evidence that Mr. Hill wanted Morgan to stay at the stable? Threatening letters? All of the above would be nice.

While I was making wishes, I could use a billion dollars and world peace.

A flash of red drew my attention to a small trash can between the two nightstands. When I pulled it out, the words

*"PAST DUE"* leaped off the page. Florence had missed three tuition payments. The total amount owed made me shudder. Thank goodness I never wanted to pursue a career in medicine. I snapped a picture before dropping the bill back in the garbage.

Next, I opened the drawer on the left nightstand. Inside, I found a hairbrush holding several short dark brown strands. This must be Florence's side. Crossing the room, I dropped to my knees and opened a drawer. It held lots of riding pants, t-shirts, and nothing else. Did Morgan keep a diary? Getting to read her innermost thoughts might be an incredible violation of her privacy, but it would be worth it to gain clues into her death.

I ran my hands over the fabric and didn't find anything. The second drawer contained socks, underwear, and bras. Buried in the far-right corner, I found a cell phone.

Curious, I pulled it out. I'd assumed Morgan's phone was with her when she'd been killed and the police took it, along with records of any texts or calls on Sunday morning. But now I wondered where a jockey put their phone while racing. If every gram of weight counted, they wouldn't want to carry it. They probably weren't allowed.

It was a small Nokia flip phone, not a smart phone. Maybe Morgan kept a spare phone around in case she needed it. It was possible that she'd never thrown away her last phone after upgrading. In that case, I'd expect the battery to be dead.

The device powered on right away. Thankfully, it wasn't password protected. There were no contacts saved, no call history, no photos. Nothing suggested Morgan kept this phone for sentimental reasons. Then I found a text conversation in the trash.

The final messages, sent Saturday, made me gasp.

Where are you? We need to talk.

I'm done. It's over.

What was over? Did Morgan break up with Bryce? If so, why didn't anyone mention it?

Curious, I scrolled back. Before Saturday, the last message was in September.





According to Bryce, he and Morgan had started dating about six months ago—long after these messages. It looked like she had been dating someone else who worked at the racetrack. When last season ended, they went their separate ways. Her boyfriend expected to rekindle the romance when the new season started, and Morgan rejected him.

Dating didn't require a devoted secret cell phone, unless her boyfriend was married.

I continued reading. Other than the breakup, the messages made no sense. Every couple of weeks, someone texted a number. That was it. No context. The highest number was twelve, but they weren't in any discernible sequence.

Morgan had been conducting a secret affair. The coded messages said when to meet at some pre-arranged location. The other party sent all the scheduling texts. Either Morgan wasn't that invested, or the person she was meeting had all the power. She never even asked to reschedule.

Then Morgan broke things off. The next day, someone killed her.

Statistically, most murdered women were victimized by a current or former partner. Morgan's boyfriend couldn't get out of bed right now, much less sneak into the stables to commit murder. But Morgan's ex might have access to the property.

The thread started halfway through the season last summer, then stopped on Labor Day. I'd have to ask Jacob when they ran the final races of the year to confirm my suspicion that Morgan and her secret boyfriend parted ways when the track closed for the winter.

If I was right, this phone showed a motive to kill Morgan. Once I found the ex, I might have the killer. Either the person she'd been seeing didn't like Morgan's decision to break up, or someone else found out about the affair. A wife, maybe. Or fellow employees.

What if Mr. Hill hadn't come to see Bryce? Maybe he'd been looking for this phone and used Bryce as a cover. There weren't many reasons to keep a secret phone for dates. But if Morgan was seeing her rich older boss, that changed everything. The final message illustrating the power dynamic between the couple supported this theory.

Morgan had never responded to the assertion that she didn't get to end the relationship. I wondered why she'd kept the phone, unless she'd wanted it for evidence.

Another motive: protecting the family. A spouse's anger. Someone worried about a sexual harassment charge. All possible.

The police needed these messages, but I couldn't tell them how I found the phone. Breaking into someone's home to search was illegal. After we got home, I'd give Doug an "anonymous" tip. He'd protect my identity, and the department would get the evidence. They might decode the rest of the messages or trace the other number.

Before leaving, I pulled out my phone and took pictures of the message thread. Then I put everything back the way I'd found it and lifted the edge of Morgan's mattress to peek beneath. Still no diary, darn it. Why couldn't she have kept a detailed journal, outlining her every move and every person who disliked her?

Footsteps pounding down the hall made me jump about three feet. The door flew open, and Jacob appeared at the threshold. "Aly! What are you doing here?"

"Uh, how did you find me?" I asked, ignoring his question.

"You asked where Florence and Morgan's room was before disappearing," he said. "How did you get in?"

"It was unlocked." Technically, not a lie. The lock *was* open after I picked it.

"Come on, we've got to go."

"What's going on?" I asked. "Is Flo coming?"

He shook his head. "Someone broke into your car."

# CHAPTER SIXTEEN

AT JACOB'S ANNOUNCEMENT, the hair on my arms stood up. "Someone broke into my car? Why?"

"I don't know, but it's going to rain again. Come on, let's go!"

I hesitated. Although someone breaking into my car was bad news, racing to the parking lot wouldn't undo it. If I stayed here, I might find more evidence. It really felt like I was onto something with this cell phone/secret lover.

"Did you see who did it?"

He shook his head. "When I left, I sat on the doorstep to watch for people coming. Then another resident walked up, so I pretended to be leaving. That's when I saw your car."

Thunder rumbled overhead. Lovely. Repairing a broken window was bad enough, but now I'd have a drenched interior. The investigation would have to wait. After locking the door so Florence wouldn't realize we'd been here, I followed Jacob.

Outside, he pointed forlornly at the side of my SUV. When I spotted the gaping hole in my rear passenger-side window, my heart sank. Part of me had hoped Jacob was joking.

How could this happen? "Is the inside soaked?"

"Nah. It looks like the rain stopped before it happened. I just hope you didn't leave anything valuable inside."

"I don't have anything valuable." I tried to sound more upbeat than I felt, but my voice shook. "Other than the car, anyway. One of the benefits of being a poor grad student."

The downside, of course, was that I didn't have extra money to fix a broken window. Nor did I have a lot of free time between work and family and investigating murders.

Swallowing a frustrated sigh, I put Olive's hat in the cargo area, away from the tempered glass. Then I grabbed another paper grocery bag and carefully filled it with the broken fragments of my window.

Jacob said, "I get it. I'd hoped Sunday's races would be my ticket into the higher-paying gigs, but it's more likely they'll send me up the river."

"Don't talk like that. We'll figure this out," I said. "We should get the police report from Bryce's accident. It might tell us something."

"Morgan was paranoid. Car accidents happen all the time," he said.

Yes, they did, but until I got a peek at Florence's car, I refused to discard this theory. If Bryce had any mundane explanation for the collision, I'd have dropped it already. But his description of the incident, while fuzzy, seemed suspicious.

"Bryce made it sound like the car was gunning for him," I said.

"Bryce was high on painkillers."

"Valid."

"Did you find anything in Flo's room?" Jacob asked.

"Maybe. Was Morgan dating anyone last season?"

"I don't know, why?"

"I found a spare cell phone."

"Can I see?"

I shook my head. "I put it back for the police to find. Taking it creates a chain of custody problem."

"Chain of what?"

"Court stuff," I said. Living with a police officer, I knew all about preserving evidence. It came up every time we watched a crime thriller. "It's not important. I have a question for you. Do jockeys take their cell phones to the track with them?"

"Some do. Phones aren't allowed on the track itself within an hour of the first race, but we have them in the stables. Some people leave them at home or in their cars. There are also lockers."

Lockers! I couldn't believe I hadn't thought of that earlier. Even if the jockeys wore their racing finery to work, they'd need to store their belongings. "Are they assigned or first come, first served?"

"It's like a gym. Grab one, put a lock on it. But mostly, we have our own spots."

"Do you know if Morgan used one?"

He shrugged. "Probably."

"Did anyone mention finding Morgan's phone after she died?"

"No, but I didn't ask. I thought you found her phone."

"It doesn't appear to be her primary number." I summarized the contents of the phone, ending with, "I think Morgan had an affair last season before she met Bryce. Do you remember seeing her with anyone else? Any furtive looks, anything like that?"

"That's not something I pay attention to," Jacob said. "Who people date is their business. I ride, I work, I train."

"Did Ryder work here last summer?"

"No, he's new. It was a big deal when he got hired. He used to work at the Kentucky Derby. Acts like he's the Second Coming."

Darn it. If Ryder wasn't the jilted lover, who was? "Can you think of anyone else it could be?"

Jacob's nose scrunched up as he considered my question. "There were rumors last summer about Mr. Hill having an affair with someone at the track. I never heard the details."

"Interesting. Is that why Morgan switched stables?" I asked. "Maybe Mr. Hill wouldn't accept the end of the relationship, so she left."

"Then he found out and killed her?" Jacob's voice grew louder with excitement. "Do you think that's why he came here? He could have been looking for her secret phone."

"You may be on to something." I sighed. "It doesn't make sense that he'd have killed Morgan to stop her from leaving. But if she dumped him and started dating Bryce, then it's personal. It fits. Mr. Hill hit Bryce's car to make him back off. When Morgan refused to start seeing Mr. Hill again, he killed her."

Jacob picked glass shards out of my back seat while I searched for a window covering. Unfortunately, the options were limited. I had some reusable grocery bags, the now-dripping feathered hat, or my shirt. Grocery bag for the win.

"Tell me more about Mr. Hill. I barely caught a glimpse of his suit."

"Ryder says he looks like Mr. Peanut. Hill's got a thin mustache, and he wears suits that cost more than my rent. He's wound tighter than a spring. That's why I was surprised to run into him. Mr. Hill keeps a firm separation between himself and us."

"Not if he's sleeping with a jockey," I said.

"Good point."

"Does he have a temper? Have you ever seen him get angry?"

"Nah. But that's what you see on the news, right?"

"It's always the quiet ones," I murmured. "He could have snapped."

"It's possible," Jacob said. He held up a handful of the glass he'd pulled out of my back seat. "I need someplace to put this."

I passed him another grocery bag so we could finish. Together, it didn't take long to clean up the mess. Taking the bags, Jacob went in search of a trash can while I started the car.

Once I climbed into the driver's seat, I noticed a scrap of paper on the dashboard. It hadn't been there earlier. Leaning over, I picked it up just as Jacob returned.

### *LEAVE IT ALONE.*

A chill went down my spine. "What is this?"

He read the note, his expression inscrutable. Finally, he said, "This was a mistake. I shouldn't have dragged you into this. Now someone wants to stop us from investigating."

"Nice try." If anything, this incident made me want to clear Jacob's name faster as revenge for my window. "If they're nervous, we must be on the right track."

"I don't know. Investigating sounded like a good idea, but we're looking for a *murderer*. We could be in danger."

"We're not going to confront anyone," I said. "We're just asking some questions. Once we get an idea of motive and some solid suspects, we'll turn everything over to the police."

"You promise?" he asked. "If you get hurt, Cal will never forgive me."

"Pinky swear." I stared at the note thoughtfully. "Who knows we're here?"

"Bryce, obviously. Mr. Hill, if he noticed us."

"Bryce couldn't have snuck down the stairs to break into my car while we were in his apartment," I said. "Especially with a broken leg."

"We're not far from the stables," Jacob said. "Anyone might have followed us."

"Who knows we're investigating?"

His face turned red. "I, uh, may have told a couple of the guys you were going to clear my name. At the stables yesterday. They're my friends!"

For the love of Newton. "How many?"

He thought for a minute. "Robert. He probably told Frank."

I sighed. "Anyone else?"

"Ken was there. He's one of the other trainers. I think he was talking to a groom. Just those four, I think. Oh! And there was a reporter. No one else. Except whoever might have overheard us."

I fought the urge to rub my temples. Typically, I didn't invite everyone I knew—including large chunks of the suspect pool—to participate in my investigations.

"Did the reporter have bright red hair?"

He shook his head. "I didn't see him. Flo told me someone from the press was nosing around, asking questions about Morgan's death."

Internally, I sighed. As investigative partners went, Jacob wasn't the most proactive. My friend Tiffaneigh would have found the reporter, pretended to be an eyewitness, and interrogated him. Jacob didn't even ask for a name. I suspected Florence had been talking about TJ, but it could've been someone from Willow Falls or even Saratoga.

"Why does it matter?" Jacob asked.

"Do you know your friends well enough to trust them with our lives?"

He dropped his head into his hands with a groan. "I'm so stupid."

"It's not your fault, but you have to remember that the killer might be someone you know. Everyone is a suspect until we've cleared them. We know the killer had access to the stable—that includes every single person you just named." I paused. "Where does Mr. Hill live?"

"Uh, a mansion? Not around here, though. He probably rented a place for the season."

Without an address, I'd have to question him at the track. Unless someone else watched us leave the stables, the only people who knew we'd come here were Mr. Hill and Bryce.

Between the broken window and the cryptic texts, Mr. Hill had become Suspect Number 1.

I sighed. "Let's see if he went back to the track."

"Are you sure you want to?" Jacob asked. "Whoever left that note seems to not appreciate us poking around. Maybe we should stop."

"That means we're getting close," I said. "Listen, I'll stay in public places. I won't confront anyone alone. Besides, the police are still investigating *you*. We need to find the truth."

He grumbled but agreed that we should at least find evidence to clear his name before giving up, regardless of whether we identified the real killer. "If Mr. Hill is at the track today, he's probably near the exercise ring. He likes to watch the horses and talk to the trainers."

Before we found his boss, Jacob led me to the jockeys' locker room, set between two restrooms. Orange lockers stretched across the wall in two rows, top and bottom. About half a dozen locks protected the contents, but most were unlocked. Curious, I reached for the nearest door and opened it. Nothing inside.

"How many people use these?" I asked.

"Almost everyone." Jacob pointed. "That's mine. The rest are mostly empty because the track's closed."

"Have any of these locks been here since Sunday? It could be Morgan's."

He nodded toward the middle of the row. "That green lock hasn't moved in years. No one knows why. People used to talk about cutting it off, but it became a good luck charm."

I sighed. "So it wasn't Morgan's?"

"I doubt it."

None of the remaining locks had anything on them to indicate who owned them. Although I could probably use my powers to open each, it didn't feel right to indiscriminately rifle through other people's stuff. There was no reason to suspect any of these locker users.

Instead, I'd poke around the places that hadn't been

locked. The top unit in the row closest to the door opened easily beneath my fingers. Inside hung a red Kansas City Chiefs sweatshirt with the number 87 on the back. "I don't suppose this belonged to Morgan?"

"That's Frank's," Jacob said.

"Wow. I was kidding. I didn't think you'd know," I said.

"He was incredibly obnoxious after the last Super Bowl. Trust me, everyone knows Frank loves the Chiefs."

"Does he leave a sweatshirt here year-round? Because 87 is not just his favorite player's number, it's the actual outside temperature."

Jacob snorted. "It gets cold in the security room with all the computer stuff. They blast the A/C."

Frank hadn't stored anything in the sweatshirt's pockets, and the locker was otherwise empty. I shut it and moved on. The lower unit had a blue padlock on it, so I skipped it.

"Are you going to check them all?" Jacob asked.

"I know it's tedious, but that's my process. Create a theory and test it. I'm a scientist, and the method works for me. Someone might have left a clue in one of these lockers. The only way to find out is to check."

Jacob moved across the room. "It'll go faster if we work together. I'll meet you in the middle."

Inside the next locker, someone had stacked what looked like dozens of cans of protein shakes, boxes of energy bars, and even packages of beef jerky.

"Hungry?" I asked Jacob.

He glanced over. "Oh, that's for everyone. Protein shakes are great for filling up without worrying about making weight."

"That's what you eat every day?"

"Most days." He moved on to the next locker in his row. "Empty."

We worked quickly and efficiently, opening each locker and examining the inside before moving on. The only sounds were the squeal of hinges and the clang of metal on metal.

About a third of the way down the row, I found a crumpled piece of paper in the back of a bottom locker. Curious, I tugged it out.

Before tossing it, I unrolled the ball and smoothed the wrinkles. It was a square piece of paper, with rows of text. The top said "NYRA," which sounded vaguely familiar. I also recognized the words "Shady Grove" and "Race 2."

I must be holding a betting ticket. Why was it in the locker room?

My heart pounded. If only I'd gotten Florence to tell me more about gambling track workers!

Jacob's voice interrupted my train of thought. "What's that?"

"You tell me." I held it out. "Looks like a betting ticket, but employees aren't allowed to bet."

He took the ticket and read it carefully. "A visitor could have brought this in. Someone on one of the tours."

"What if it was a track worker? Can we look up who bought a specific ticket?"

"I don't think so. Is it important?"

"It could be, if Morgan caught someone breaking the rules," I said, thinking of Florence's comment.

"I guess that's why Cal asked you to help," he said. "I'd have chucked it. C'mon, let's see what else we can find."

We resumed our search, but I kept wondering how a betting ticket made it into an area only accessible to track employees. Our tour group never came in here. Even if another one did, why toss the ticket in a locker instead of the garbage? If I'd found this earlier, I wouldn't have given it a second thought. But after Florence's slip, the ticket was too big a coincidence to ignore.

# CHAPTER SEVENTEEN

AFTER THE REST of the lockers turned up nothing of interest, Jacob and I walked to the parking lot. Only a few vehicles remained. To my relief, Jacob gestured toward a shiny car in the spot nearest the stable. "That's Mr. Hill's car. He must have come back."

Finally, a break! I made a split second decision. "Excellent! Where do you think he is?"

Jacob opened his mouth to say something, then seemed to reconsider. Finally, he asked, "You're not going to accuse Mr. Hill of murder, are you? Cal will never forgive me if I get his girlfriend killed."

"You know, that sounds like an excellent way to get banned from the track, but I'll pass." I waved him away. "Go home. I'll be fine. We'll talk tomorrow."

He looked skeptical but directed me toward the ring where Mr. Hill might be supervising the trainers before saying goodbye. Anxious to beat the next storm burst, I started over there immediately.

How did I convince Mr. Hill to talk to me? If I accused him of having an affair with a jockey and killing her, he'd call security. In the past, I'd pretended to be writing a story for the school newspaper to interview people, so that might work.

While I followed Jacob's directions, I practiced my spiel. By the time I arrived at the exercise ring, I almost believed I was researching a story for the college paper. A man in a pin-striped suit stood by one of the railings, one foot placed casually on the lowest rung. Inside the ring, two riders took their mounts through the paces. A dark-haired man I didn't recognize stood near the center.

Tentatively, I moved toward the man outside the ring. If I'd had any questions about this guy's identity, Ryder's description answered them. Personally, I thought he looked more like the bad guy in *Titanic* than Mr. Peanut, but he wore a pin-striped suit. A monocle and top hat wouldn't have seemed out of place.

When Mr. Hill saw me step through the doorway, he straightened and placed his foot on the ground, as if relaxation time had ended. "Can I help you?"

My well-practiced opening flew out of my head, and words started tripping over themselves to race out of my nervous mouth. "Hi, Mr. Hill! My name's Aly Reynolds. I'm a friend of Jacob Brunner's, the jockey."

His eyes swept up and down my yoga pants and t-shirt. His upper lip curled distastefully before he caught himself. "Hello. This is a private area. I'd recommend calling your friend after his shift."

"Actually, I was looking for you. I'm writing a public interest piece for the college paper. Would it be okay if I asked you a few questions? About racing? I love racing. It's so fascinating!"

His initial wariness faded. "Yes, certainly! I love seeing young people taking an interest in the sport. It's got such a rich tradition. What would you like to know?"

I pulled out my phone and studied the screen as if I'd written interview questions on it. To ease him into the conversation, I started with several softball questions like "How many horses do you own?"

He was more than happy to talk about his stable while I

took notes.

Finally, I gathered up my courage. "Tell me about Morgan Gunderson's death."

His expression softened. "What a tragedy. Although accidents happen in racing, it's always a shock to lose someone so young. Especially in a case like this. Hill Stables is covering all of her funeral costs."

Interesting that money would be his initial focus. He didn't speak like someone who had lost someone they knew intimately, but he wouldn't be transparent with a total stranger. I also noticed that he didn't mention murder. Homicide wasn't great for business.

"That's very kind of you, sir." I took a deep breath. "I heard that someone killed Morgan. Why would anyone hurt a jockey? Do you think someone wanted to prevent her from winning?"

"I'm sure I have no idea."

"Someone said another owner wanted to lure her away. Do you think she refused to go?"

"I don't engage in idle gossip. While Morgan was a talented rider, there are many qualified jockeys. Losing one certainly wouldn't justify murder. At least not in my mind."

Not in mine, either, but that wasn't the point.

"You seem like a great boss," I said, playing to his ego. "What about Mr. O'Brien? Was he equally pragmatic, or would he get angry if Morgan rejected a job offer?"

"I'm sure he would have gotten over it. If you want to know about Gavin O'Brien, I suggest you speak with him. Is that all your questions for me?"

"Just one more." While gathering my nerve, I pretended to consult my notes. Then I took a deep breath. "Did you and Morgan have an intimate relationship?"

Mr. Hill stared at me so intently I could hardly breathe. "What?"

"Forgive me, but there are rumors, sir, that Morgan was

having an affair with someone at the track." I didn't add that any such rumors originated with me within the past half hour. "Someone very powerful."

Mr. Hill's face turned red. His shoulders shook. I inched away from him, worried he might lunge at me. Then he threw back his head and laughed. I glanced around uncertainly. Should I go? What was happening?

The dark-haired man came over and took Mr. Hill's hand, whispering in his ear. He doubled over, laughing too hard to even acknowledge the newcomer.

The stranger turned to me. "What did you say to him?"

"I, uh, asked if he was sleeping with one of his jockeys."

The man pulled himself upright and turned toward Mr. Hill. "Excuse me? Were you?"

"Oh, no. No, no." Mr. Hill wiped tears from his eyes. "Gary, this girl thinks I had an affair with the girl who died."

Gary snorted. "Fat chance."

I took in the energy between them, the familiarity… and the matching gold wedding bands. "You two are married."

"For nearly twenty years," Mr. Hill said proudly. "We were one of the first couples to tie the knot when it became legal."

"Together for years before that," Gary said.

"I haven't dated a woman since high school," Mr. Hill said. "What brought you to this extremely amusing conclusion?"

I shook my head. "People hinted that someone killed Morgan because of a big secret. Then I found something… it doesn't matter. I'm sorry for wasting your time."

"You didn't tell me you were involved in the case," Mr. Hill said.

"Aren't you young to be a cop?" Gary asked.

"I'm not," I said. "Just gathering information. Um, for the paper, like I said."

"Someone is having fun with you if they pointed the

finger at Drummond," Gary said. "We spent the entire weekend at the Clubhouse. There are dozens of videos and social media posts. We gave the camera footage to Officer Matthews last weekend."

"You have camera footage?" I asked.

"Not from the stables," Mr. Hill said. "But everywhere else. Whoever knocked out the cameras only targeted that area."

If Morgan's affair hadn't been with her boss, who was it?

After I apologized again, I left. Doug could verify the Hills' information, and there was no one else to question. The few people who'd been working had mostly left. I wanted to ask Florence about the ticket, but I hadn't seen her since Jacob and I returned.

Florence wouldn't talk to me, anyway. She needed to want to tell me her secrets. My best bet was to go home, review what we knew, and pick up the investigation in the morning.

Meanwhile, I needed to fix my window. The rain had stopped for now, but I didn't want to leave my SUV parked outside overnight with a hole in the glass covered with only a soggy paper bag.

Luckily, this gave me an opportunity to ask our local mechanic about Flo's car. It might still be at the shop! Now that Mr. Hill had dropped down my suspect list, it was time to get to the bottom of Florence's strange behavior.

I called Kind of a Big Wheel, and the owner answered. Mike told me they couldn't fix my window tonight, but if I dropped it off, he'd look first thing in the morning.

The mechanic's shop wasn't far from Second Street, where my brother Kevin owned a law office, so leaving my car shouldn't be an issue. It only took a second to confirm that yes, Kevin was still working, and he'd take me home.

After parking at the shop, I went to the back seat to grab my stuff before going inside. With a start, I realized what had been bothering me since leaving Bryce's place.

Last night after getting home from Missing Pieces, I'd put

the borrowed (now clean) dress into a small black backpack and put it on my back seat. The hat had been on top. I'd planned to return everything the next time I went to work.

The hat sat where I'd tossed it, feather drooping after the rain but trying to stand proud. Nothing else.

The bag was gone.

# CHAPTER EIGHTEEN

ON SUNDAY EVENING, I'd washed the outfit Olive loaned me for the track, folded it, and put it in a backpack on my front seat. I'd forgotten to take it inside Missing Pieces, so it went into the back when Jacob joined me in the vehicle. I was absolutely positive. Now, the bag was gone.

The note told me this wasn't a random smash-and-grab. Someone wanted to scare me away from investigating Morgan's death. So why take the bag?

The bag didn't look expensive. Thousands of people owned a small black backpack. Even Cal had one.

Now that I thought about it, Cal brought his backpack to the track on Sunday. It held his camera equipment.

During the races, he took probably two hundred pictures, clicking away the entire time. Maybe he unknowingly captured something important. When Cal texted Jacob after the final race, he'd handed me his camera. I'd taken a picture of the security guards. Anyone seeing us on Sunday after Morgan's death might think I owned the camera, not Cal. Especially with what looked like his camera bag in my back seat.

We needed to go through those pictures.

Before heading to the mechanic's, I texted Cal.

The message remained unread. After a minute, I tried again.





Still nothing.

When I locked my phone, the date and time flashed across the screen. Right. Cal worked on campus as a research assistant, even over the summer. Although Professor Ng was traveling, Cal had agreed to review and catalog specimens remotely. He'd be working, and Cal never took his phone into the lab. It could be hours before he saw my texts.

I shook my head at my folly. Whoever broke into my car might have wanted something to sell. Maybe they broke in to warn me off and then decided to grab whatever they saw lying around. I might be making macromolecules out of atoms.

Even if someone wanted the camera, Cal would be safe on campus. The killer couldn't know where he was. I sent yet another text apologizing for the unnecessary urgency and asking him to call me when he finished work, then set my GPS for Kind of a Big Wheel.

Ten minutes later, I stood beside a Black guy a few years older than me. Mike was medium height, with long braids in his black hair. He surveyed my window solemnly. "Did you get mad at your car?"

"Sadly, no. I left a backpack on the seat and someone thought it was valuable." I sighed and shook my head. "Joke's on them. Can you fix it?"

"Yeah, sure." Mike named a price as we walked inside the shop.

He took all my information before printing a form and handing it over for signing. The estimate made me cringe. Good thing I could eat at my brother's house to save money on food.

"Hey, um, did you work on my friend's car?" I asked after handing over my keys. "Florence. She raved about the guy she talked to. Said he was absolutely the best."

"Oh, yeah? That's nice of her. Florence? I don't remember anyone by that name."

"She said you were cute, too," I said, figuring it wouldn't hurt to flatter him. I described her, then said, "She was here Sunday morning."

Mike thought for a minute. "Tall girl, about your age? Real thin?"

"Yeah, that's her. She was impressed with your work."

"It was nothing. Anyone can replace a starter."

Starter?

"I thought she needed body work. Broken headlights or front bumper damage, maybe?"

"No, the car looked new. Your friend took good care of it, but she needed a new starter." He rubbed his chin thoughtfully. "That girl said I was cute? I never would've guessed. She barely looked at me."

"Some people are shy," I said.

"It's not that. She was on her phone, crying about a guy who didn't like her. He'd been in an accident. When I finished her car, she took off," Mike said. "Sounded like she was going to see him."

My eyes widened. When Flo first mentioned Bryce, her reaction had seemed strange. Then Bryce said she hated him, and I'd figured that was it. Now, it sounded like Florence was in love with her best friend's boyfriend.

If Florence was jealous enough of Morgan to kill her, it didn't make sense that she'd have hit Bryce's car first. Not to mention, her front end was perfect. Morgan's death couldn't be related to the car accident if Florence was involved. Maybe Bryce's accident was what it looked like—a driver running a red light.

Could Florence's cell phone have been hidden on Morgan's side of the room? Maybe she and Bryce were dating. No, that didn't make sense. The phone's owner initiated the breakup. What was I missing?

Mike had finished the work on Florence's car early enough for her to return to the stables, and if she'd gone to the dorms, she'd have been close enough to sneak in and attack Morgan. Seems like it would be easier to kill her pretty much any other time, since they lived together, but strong emotions weren't rational.

After thanking Mike, I left, still considering his comments. Clearly, I'd missed something. Florence lied about her feelings for her best friend's boyfriend, but maybe she thought it would be in poor taste to talk about it. Why didn't Bryce tell us she'd visited? If they killed Morgan together, he could have called Florence and sent her to break into my car. But— why?

The killer wouldn't have warned me off the case unless we were getting close. Someone thought Jacob and I were on the verge of finding something important. I wished they'd tell me what.

# CHAPTER NINETEEN

BEFORE HEADING to my brother's office, I swung by the *Shady Grove Sentinel* to see TJ. He'd been investigating something at the racetrack on Sunday; maybe we could share information.

The newspaper office wasn't far from Missing Pieces, on the top floor of a three-story office building that also housed a couple of smaller offices and Mayor Banister's re-election headquarters. Given my relationship with our local politician, I resisted the urge to make a rude gesture on my way to the elevator.

Other than TJ, the *Sentinel* had two full-time employees: his father, editor-in-chief, and all-around nice guy, Hal Crews, and his ninety-year-old assistant, Ethel. She thought TJ walked on water and hadn't understood why I took offense to the articles he'd written about me.

When I opened the double glass doors separating the office from the elevator bank on the top floor, Ethel scowled at me. If looks could kill, I'd be joining Morgan in the morgue.

"I come in peace," I said.

"Oh, yeah? Is harassing my boy peace?"

Given that TJ was older than me, it seemed odd to hear

her describing him as her boy. "I'm not here to harass anyone. I want to talk to TJ about a story."

She gave me the side-eye. "What kind of story?"

"I ran into him at the racetrack on Sunday, around lunchtime."

"At the track? That's interesting. TJ never goes to the races."

If Ethel didn't know that TJ was meeting an informant, I wasn't going to enlighten her. "I figured he was doing a puff piece about horse racing."

She snorted. "Puff pieces aren't really TJ's strong suit."

"Agreed," I said. "Anyway, he wrote the article about Morgan's death. The jockey."

"You got something to add?"

"I won't know until I talk to him. Can I go in?"

Ethel grunted. "Let me ask if he wants to see you."

She picked up her phone and pushed a few buttons, spinning around so I wouldn't hear her. When she finished, she replaced the receiver and turned back to her computer.

"Was that a yes?" I asked. "Can I see him?"

She continued working. I was about to call TJ when a door opened and he emerged. He walked toward me with a broad smile. "Aly! Let's talk at my desk."

He ushered me through the glass doors to his computer station. I welcomed the opportunity to get out from under Ethel's gaze.

When we reached his desk, TJ sat in the chair and gestured toward a small black chair nearby. "How can I help you?"

"What were you warning me about at the track on Sunday?" I asked, getting directly to the point.

TJ's eyes narrowed. "Why are you asking?"

I ticked the reasons off on my fingers. "First, you were at the track for no apparent reason. You gave me cryptic warnings about not getting involved in something. No idea what. A girl got murdered, and her roommate accidentally mentions a track employee gambling. Then I find something interesting. What was Morgan wrapped up in?"

"Why do you care?"

"My boyfriend's cousin argued with Morgan that morning in front of a lot of people. He also sent an angry text about getting rid of her, and now the police think he was involved. I want to clear his name."

TJ sighed and rubbed his head. "If I tell you what I know, will you reciprocate?"

"As long as you promise not to directly quote me in your article or imply that I killed Morgan."

He laughed. "Fair enough. Listen, I don't know anything concrete yet. I never got confirmation for my story. Someone sent an anonymous tip about a scheme at the track. They told me to stand by the railing near the front of the stable and someone would meet me. When I arrived, people were milling around everywhere. The only one I recognized was you. That's why I said hello. I thought you might be my contact."

"Me? Why me?"

"You always know things." He shrugged. "Why not you?"

I couldn't answer that. "Does that mean you didn't talk to anyone?"

"No one showed up. I called and texted, but they never replied," TJ said. "Then the police called me this morning."

Something clicked. "Was Morgan your source?"

"Yeah. The sheriff asked why I'd sent her so many messages shortly before she died." He shook his head. "I didn't know it was her. Whatever she wanted to tell me, she never got the chance."

"You don't have any idea?" My mind went to the hidden phone. The numbers. "Track employees are prohibited from betting on the races. A vet's assistant said someone does it, anyway. Then I found a ticket stuffed in an employee locker at the track."

"Yeah? Good work. Can I see it?"

I patted my pockets a few times before concluding the ticket must have fallen out in my car. "I'll text you a picture later. Did your source hint at who she was talking about? Morgan wouldn't rat herself out."

"Maybe she wasn't acting alone."

Morgan's words rang in my head. *It's over.*

She was finished with the scheme. Someone pressured her into betting on that race. For whatever reason, she believed that she was going to walk away.

I pulled out my phone. The last texts before the sender asked to meet Morgan, had seemed meaningless.

2

No.

I'd thought the numbers were times, but they must refer to races. The date must be when the message was sent. The horse was also known: whichever one Morgan rode in the given race. She bet on herself. Or a friend bet on her.

Finally, we were getting somewhere. Someone wanted Morgan to bet on herself to win the second race. She'd initially refused. When they said she wasn't allowed to quit, she'd called the newspapers to make the scheme public. Then Morgan's partner killed her to keep her quiet.

Why was that specific race so important? Did they rig it? A guaranteed payoff would offset the risk of getting fired. Morgan's horse was the favorite to win that race, though. Unless they put down a lot of money, how big a payout did she expect?

I couldn't tell TJ about my vision, but he might answer some questions. "How do you rig a horse race? Aren't there about a million factors involved?"

"Probably. Even if you disable the favorite, there are ten other horses to beat. One person couldn't make them all sick without calling attention to themselves."

"Exactly. What about some kind of horse steroids?"

"Nah, they test for that," TJ said. "You said your friend's a jockey, right? He might know. See if he'll give me a quote for my article."

"I'll ask. Hold on, there's more." Pulling out my phone, I scrolled to the screenshots I'd taken of the texts. "Look at this. I found a secret phone in Morgan's room with these cryptic messages. I thought she was meeting someone for an affair, but now—"

"She's talking to her partner in crime," TJ finished. "Who is it?"

"No idea. Can you trace the number?"

"I sure can." TJ sat at his computer and began typing. I read the phone number aloud. He punched it in, pushed a few buttons, and sighed. "It's a VoIP number. Free line obtained online. Could belong to anyone."

"What about the phone I found? Can we confirm it's Morgan's?"

He shrugged. "I'll try."

Again, I read him the number. After punching it in, he shook his head. "Nothing. They're probably both burner phones."

Of course they were. Completely untraceable.

Just when I thought we were finally getting somewhere, the door slammed shut in my face. This killer had us chasing our tails, and I didn't like it one bit.

# CHAPTER TWENTY

ON MY WAY OUT, I stopped at the editor-in-chief's office to speak with Hal, the man who'd written so many articles about Penny's murder. He might be willing to talk about the case. I had no doubt he'd remember it.

Hal's face told me exactly how TJ would look in twenty years. They had the same blue eyes, oval face, and pug nose. Only their hair differed. TJ kept his cropped close to his head and wore a goatee. Hal was clean-shaven and allowed his red curls free rein over his head.

When Hal saw me in the doorway, he beamed and beckoned me inside the office. Although large in square footage, the room felt tiny due to the stacks of paper covering every available surface, including both visitor chairs. I wouldn't be surprised if he had original copies of the Penny and Tripp articles here somewhere.

"Aly! What a coincidence!" he said. "I was planning to drop by Missing Pieces later today."

"Oh, yeah? I'm working this afternoon. Are you looking for anything specific?"

"Actually, I was looking for you."

"Alas," I said with mock sadness. "I am not for sale."

He chuckled. "Consuela at the library told me you're

interested in Penny Langley's murder. She said you printed out my articles from back then. I'm flattered."

"Does Consuela normally tell you when someone reads old newspapers?"

"I don't know. This might be the first time. Can I ask why you're researching the case?"

Although Hal's coverage made it impossible to tell what he personally thought about the case, I decided not to reveal the driving force behind my curiosity. Still, he might be able to answer a question. I didn't understand how I got the puka shell necklace if Tripp was wearing it when Penny died.

"We got a donation with a necklace Olive thought Tripp was wearing when he was arrested. I was trying to find a picture, and then I got curious."

"What was it?"

"A couple of thick black threads holding white seashells. Olive called it a puka."

"Ah, yes. I remember that. He wore it when arrested, but it wasn't introduced as evidence at trial." He turned to his computer and started clicking. "People mock my system, but this is why I never delete anything."

"You have files from thirty years ago?"

"Never means never. I always think 'what if I need it?' My wife says it's ridiculous. Now I can tell her I've been right all along." He continued scanning the screen. I was starting to think this was pointless when he leaned forward. "A-ha! The police inventoried one puka shell necklace after they arrested Tripp. Someone must have decided it didn't have any evidentiary value, because they returned it when the judge released Tripp on bail."

"They let people charged with murder out on bail?"

He shrugged. "If you're rich, white, and well-known in the community, they do."

Right. Unfair yet correct.

"Thanks, Hal. You're a gem. Shady Grove is lucky to have

you." A thought struck me. "Have you ever considered running for office?"

"What? Me becoming a politician? Heavens, no. I thought you had a higher opinion of me than that."

I snorted. "That's just it. Our local politicians are not good people. You are. Mayor Banister has been running this town for years, and she's so crooked she can't even lie in bed straight. Sheriff Matthews is her lapdog. Both of them need to go. No one runs against them."

"I hope you're not suggesting I enter law enforcement at my age. Your friend Doug would be a much better candidate."

"He won't go against his uncle." I shook my head. "No, I want you to run for mayor."

Hal weighed my words carefully. One of the things I liked about him was that he considered people's opinions. "I'm not ready to leave the newspaper business yet, but it's something to think about when I retire."

"Do you plan to retire before November?"

He laughed. "Heavens, no! Why do you want the mayor out?"

"A year ago, she had the sheriff arrest Olive for a crime she didn't commit just to close the case." Earl Parker's death was one of many events that took place in both my original world and this one, since it was unrelated to Katrina's death. I'd been around, even though living on campus. "Then, last spring, Sheriff Matthews thought I murdered someone to star in the spring play. Me! Why would I kill someone to do *more* public speaking?"

"I appreciate your faith in me, but I'm sure they believed they were doing the right thing. Sheriff Matthews didn't arrest you for killing Ms. Peters, did he?"

"No." This came out sullenly, as if I wanted to have been taken to jail to prove my point. "They're still evil."

"Why don't you ask your brother? He's pretty popular around here these days."

After I nearly got killed in a fire a few months ago, my brother sprang into action, organizing a volunteer firefighting unit in town. It had gotten a lot of interest, possibly because there was nothing else to do around here.

"He wouldn't abandon the volunteers right after putting everything together," I said. "Besides, he wants to spend as much time as possible with Katrina now that she's back. In a few years, maybe, but now, I've got my eye on you."

"I'm very flattered." Hal's ears turned pink at my praise. "Sorry, Aly. I couldn't run for mayor if I wanted to. Neither can Kevin, for that matter. The filing deadline passed months ago."

That sounded suspiciously convenient. "How do you know that?"

"I'm a newspaper man. It's my job to know everything about the town. Whether or not you like the candidates, elections are big news. I could bore you with election minutiae until your ears fall off."

"Try it, and you'll hear way more than you ever needed to know about the periodic table." I smiled sadly. "Thanks, anyway."

"You don't need me. Manuel Diaz threw his hat in the ring this year. First time anyone has opposed Beth Banister in ages."

The name rang a faint bell. "Manuel Diaz, the town comptroller?"

"One and the same," Hal said. "I believe he's also the town clerk, registrar of deeds, and tax assessor."

"Among other things." I laughed. "Is he going to do all that and be mayor?"

"For his sake, I hope not."

"Why haven't I heard about this?"

"With only one candidate from each party, the primary was a formality this year. No need to campaign. The election is in a few months, so he's starting to ramp up. It's not like the presidential cycle where people run constantly."

"Thank goodness," I said. "What's Manuel like? I've only met him once." That meeting occurred in an alternate universe. He could be a completely different person in this world, but I'd liked him then.

Hal said, "He's essentially run all the town services for ten years. He's known for being a thoughtful decision-maker, thorough, extremely patient, and reasonable."

"That's great, but is he evil?"

Hal laughed, although I wasn't joking. "No. He's a good man. Won Citizen of the Year a few years ago."

"He's not Mayor Banister, *and* he's a nice guy? He's got my vote!" While it may seem cavalier to have such loose voting standards, my nephew's pet turtle would have been preferable to the woman currently doing the job. "Sorry to waste your time."

"Not at all. It's always a pleasure."

When I left the newspaper office, my footsteps felt lighter. If Manual became our next mayor, Shady Grove's biggest problem would be solved.

WHEN KEVIN LEARNED that Tripp Kavanaugh's belongings had been donated to Missing Pieces, he'd been excited. He thought people would pay good money for "memorabilia." Personally, ick. I couldn't profit off someone's death, and Olive agreed. But still, Kevin studied the case in law school, and he'd have thoughts about who committed the crime. He also had a unique ability that would be invaluable if I could convince him to use it.

Kevin was locking up when I arrived. "I thought you wanted me to pick you up at the auto shop."

"The rain stopped, so I walked," I said as we went to the parking lot. "Listen, I want you to visit Tripp with me."

No matter what random things I said to him, my brother

never appeared flustered. Probably what made him such a successful lawyer. "Why?"

I described my vision and subsequent visit with Lucy. "She's positive her son didn't do it."

"Aly, please tell me you're not getting involved in yet another murder case."

To be fair, I had become involved in *two* murder cases since I last saw him, so the truthful answer was no. I had not started investigating *one other* murder. As a lawyer, my brother might appreciate the logic, but since I needed his help, it was better to be honest.

Unless I spoke my truth, Kevin would know, anyway. That was why I'd come to him: My brother could see lies.

Finally, I said, "I told Lucy that I need to believe Tripp didn't kill Penny. I'm not going to try to exonerate a guilty man."

"Why do I sense a 'but' coming?" Kevin asked as he turned toward his neighborhood.

"I have no idea who did it." I took a deep breath. "You studied the case. What do you think?"

Kevin focused on the road while he pondered my question. "I don't know. He certainly had a motive. Everyone said he was upset about the breakup."

"Can confirm. I saw them together in my vision. But a motive doesn't equal guilt."

"I'm aware of that," he said. "He also had opportunity. He was with Penny when she died. No one disputed that."

My spirits deflated. "You think he killed her?"

Kevin shook his head. "I'm not sure. The official story doesn't make sense. Where did the murder weapon go? If Tripp handed it off to someone through the window, who? They didn't charge an accomplice, and no one testified to helping."

"They wouldn't, would they?"

"For immunity, they might. Prosecutors work out deals all the time."

An excellent point. "Who were the other suspects?"

"Penny had started seeing someone new a few weeks earlier. He saw her go up the stairs with Tripp. But it was an enormous event. Pi Gamma Psi parties always drew a crowd, and the high school kids flooded in to celebrate their graduation. There are dozens of alternate suspects."

"Did any of them have a motive?"

"No one that was investigated. The police didn't look at anyone but Tripp. You can't find a motive if you're not looking for one."

"What does your gut tell you?" I asked.

"It changes on any given day. I can see the arguments on both sides."

I took a deep breath, then repeated my earlier request. "I was hoping you would go to the prison and ask him if he killed Penny."

"No."

The immediate refusal didn't surprise me. Kevin thought it wasn't fair to use his ability against criminal defendants (even, apparently, those who had already been convicted). But I didn't give up. "You said there's a whole online community of people glued to this case. They spend hours debating Tripp's guilt or innocence. If you help me figure out that truth, you'd be a hero!"

"Wrong. If you figure out the truth, *you* will be a hero. No one can know about my ability. They wouldn't believe it, anyway."

I'd hoped my brother's interest in the case and love of the truth would make it easier to convince him to help. "Come on. It's one conversation."

"He's in prison three hours away. You're not asking for a quick chat."

"What about Mom?" I asked.

He glanced at me. "What about her?"

"She says our powers are gifts, and we need to use them

to help people. That's why I'm doing this. That's why I've helped with so many cases."

"I help people, too. Lawyers help people. I use my abilities every day."

A heavy sigh escaped me as he turned the corner and his house came into sight. Part of me hated when he wouldn't use his superpowers to help me fight crime, but Kevin believed it wasn't fair. Criminal defendants had a constitutional right not to incriminate themselves, even by talking to psychics. He only took civil cases.

"What if we tell Tripp the truth?"

"Were you drinking at the track?"

"Not the *whole* truth. Let's tell him we're going to investigate, but you'll only help if you believe he's innocent. We'll say you want to hear his side of the story directly. We can tell him you're some kind of great deception expert. It's technically true."

"He'd never believe it." Kevin parked in his garage and shut off the car. "I assume you're staying for dinner. Texted Katrina earlier. One of us will take you home later."

"Don't worry about it. I'll have Cal pick me up after work."

The change in subject told me our conversation was over. People joked about lawyers being lousy people, but Kevin cared about doing the right thing. If I kept pushing, he'd dig in and refuse to budge.

Sure, I could say he owed me for all the free baby-sitting or bringing his wife back to life that one time but guilting him felt gross. Those things weren't about getting rewarded. Kevin needed to want to help.

Usually I ate at Kevin's house on Thursdays, but I didn't mind seeing my family twice in three days. Dinner was one of the highlights of my week, as it gave me a chance to spend time not only with my brother but his wife and their five-year-old son, Kyle.

Murder wasn't an appropriate dinner topic when eating

with a small child, so we kept the conversation light. Kyle told us about summer camp, and Katrina caught us up on some local gossip.

When we finished eating, Kevin put Kyle to bed while I did the dishes and Katrina got dessert ready. Once we settled down to enjoy our strawberry shortcake, I seized my opportunity.

"Katrina, did Kevin tell you that Lucretia Kavanaugh asked me to prove her son's innocence?"

Her brow wrinkled. "The case you mentioned a few months ago? The guy who killed his girlfriend at a frat party?"

"Yeah. His mother is positive he didn't do it," I said.

Briefly, I explained my vision and subsequent conversation with Lucy. Kevin watched me warily but said nothing.

"That poor woman," Katrina said. "Are you going to help?"

"I want to. No matter who the killer is, I could bring Lucy peace by telling her what happened." I waited until my brother had taken a big bite of shortcake to continue. "All I need is for Kevin to ask Tripp if he did it."

"Ooh, great idea!" Katrina said.

I beamed. I knew she'd be on my side.

"Terrible idea," Kevin said around a mouthful of whipped cream. Once he swallowed, he continued, "My ability tells me when someone is lying, but Tripp's defense was that he didn't *remember* killing Penny. Now, based on what Aly told me—he doesn't. She's essentially confirmed that he didn't lie. How could me going down there help? If he doesn't know what happened, it's impossible for me to get it out of him."

"Give yourself a little credit, dear," Katrina said. "You're a skilled litigator. Maybe a conversation with you will help him uncover some buried memory."

Kevin glanced at me. "Did you put her up to this?"

I raised my hands in defense. "I swear we didn't plan this. Look at it this way. If someone tampered with the necklace to remove a key part of the memories, talking to Tripp could fill in the blanks."

"It's more likely that his memories are incomplete," Kevin said. "He might have repressed the murder even if he did it."

"Come on, please?"

He shook his head. "I'm sorry, Aly. I'm swamped right now. My power doesn't work over the phone, and I don't have time to drive out to the Fishkill state prison. Excuse me. I have work to do."

Before I could argue further, he took his plate to the sink, kissed Katrina, and headed for the room serving as his home office.

I dropped my head into my hands. "That didn't go well."

"I'll talk to him," Katrina said. "He worries about you. He thinks investigating a murder puts us all in danger."

"Even if the killer is in jail?" Since my powers had developed, I'd found myself in a few sticky situations. No one had, to my knowledge, ever threatened Kevin's family. I'd never endanger them.

"We don't know that Tripp's the murderer. Even if he is, he may have friends on the outside."

"Can't you protect us?" One of Katrina's spells saved my life last Christmas, and she'd made my handy sunglasses of invisibility.

"To some extent. I'm not invincible, and neither are you. Not even with one of my spells. Remember that. If I die, the magic goes away." Standing up, she poured two mugs of coffee before bringing me one. "That said, his reasoning is sound. Questioning a witness who remembers nothing isn't useful. See what you find. Once you have more information, Kevin may change his mind."

"Thanks for trying." I sighed and got up to clear our dessert dishes. "Hey, do you have the paper from last weekend?"

One of my brother's quirks was that he still subscribed to a daily print newspaper. Katrina pointed toward a basket in the living room. After a moment's thought, I grabbed the Sunday and Monday papers before sitting down with my coffee to read.

In Sunday's edition, TJ covered Bryce's car accident. He didn't embellish much. The article said Bryce was driving home when a dark-colored SUV ran a red light and T-boned him. His car spun out, landing in the northbound lane facing southbound. The other driver fled the scene. There were no witnesses, and the intersection had no cameras. A coincidence, or had Morgan been right?

Monday's article covering Morgan's death didn't include many details. TJ didn't mention the cause of death, nor did he say he'd been at the track when it happened. While a good reporter wouldn't insert themselves into a story, it surprised me that TJ hadn't. Maybe there was hope for him.

I was reviewing the articles for the third time, scouring for clues, when Cal called.

"Is everything okay?" he asked the moment I answered.

"Hey! Yeah, sorry for the million texts. Did you take any pictures of Morgan on Sunday?"

"Yeah, sure. I shot all the races. I haven't gone through them yet."

After a frustrating day of dead ends, I was determined to find something, anything, to help me clear Jacob's name. My gut said there might be something important on Cal's camera. "Can you get the camera and pick me up at Kevin's? We can use Rusty's computer."

"No need. I brought it to play with the imaging software in the computer lab before work. I'll see you in twenty."

# CHAPTER TWENTY-ONE

IT DIDN'T TAKE LONG to catch Cal up on everything Jacob and I learned at the track. When I got to the vision in Wind Walker's stall, Cal deflated a bit. He didn't say so, but I knew he'd hoped my vision would show the murder's identity.

Besides being my roommate, Rusty owned a high-quality camera with a telephoto lens and other bells and whistles. He also had a computer with three enormous screens that allowed us to blow up the images and study every detail. Before I moved in, the desk had been in what became my bedroom. Now the equipment occupied the dining room table where anyone could use it. We usually ate while watching TV, anyway.

Rusty plugged Cal's camera into his computer and transferred the images before offering me the chair.

My heart sank when I saw the folder's contents. Cal had taken 372 photos at the track.

"Reviewing every single picture is going to take all year," I said.

"How do you eat an elephant?" Rusty asked.

"One bite at a time," I grumbled.

The first dozen or so images showed the front of the racetrack. I scrutinized them but didn't see anything useful. Then we got to the tour.

"There's Morgan." Cal pointed to an image where she stood in the background, talking to a big guy with his back to us. Interestingly, an upright metal bucket sat near her feet. "There's Ryder. In about ten seconds, she's going to storm off."

Morgan stood with her arms crossed, glaring at Ryder. In contrast, there was no tension in his posture. Ryder slouched against a post, hands in his pockets. I'd have given anything to have heard their conversation.

"Hold on. I'm going to rename this so I can find it again," I said. The image probably wasn't important, but we needed to mark every glimpse of Morgan.

We sifted quietly until I came upon a shot of me standing near the rail, looking out over the field. It was a full-body shot, taken from at least a few feet away.

"When did you take this?" I asked.

Cal glanced at it. "When I placed our bets before we got lunch. I wanted to test my zoom. Pretty good, huh?"

"Very good."

Leaning forward, I examined the background. TJ's red hair helped me find him. As he'd told me, he stood alone. No one was talking to him.

Cal tapped the image. "Look who else is at the railing."

We enlarged the image further, leaning so close my nose almost touched the screen.

"That's Morgan! The police said she was TJ's source, but she never showed. I didn't realize how close she came to telling him her secret."

"She's not looking at TJ."

Now that he mentioned it, her eyes were wide. Morgan's face mirrored a child who'd been caught doing something they weren't supposed to. She gazed at something beyond the edge of the picture. Given the direction, it couldn't be TJ.

"What's she afraid of?" I asked.

"Good question." He clicked backward, but we didn't find anything useful.

The next several pictures were wide crowd shots with dozens of people. No matter how hard I looked, nothing jumped out. Then Cal had taken a picture of the betting windows. At least forty people stood between him and the front of the line, including someone in a familiar red sweatshirt.

"Hold on," I said. "Can you zoom in on that guy?"

"You think being a Chiefs fan makes him a killer?"

I snorted. "Hardly. But he's wearing a sweatshirt with a hood over his face in July, he's tilted toward Morgan, *and* I saw that exact hoodie in the locker room."

"The Chiefs are pretty popular," Cal said doubtfully. "A ton of people have Kelce sweatshirts."

"How many of them wear it when it's as hot as last Sunday?"

"Good point." He zoomed in. The man was Frank's size, towering over the nearby patrons. He stood stiffly, hands curled into fists. And his attention was unmistakably focused on something over by the railing. "He saw Morgan near TJ."

"I think so," I said.

"Why would he care about Morgan talking to a reporter?"

Only one reason came to mind. He knew what she planned to say, and he didn't like it.

Frank was in the stable when Morgan died. He'd said someone unplugged the security system. Who better to sabotage the cameras than the guy who monitored them?

A chill went down my spine when I remembered Jacob had told Robert I was helping him investigate Morgan's death. Frank probably also knew by now. He'd been at the track not long before someone broke into my car. He could've followed us and left the note.

Frank also had access to the locker room, where I'd found that betting ticket. We knew he'd been in there, thanks to the red sweatshirt. He'd used the hood to cover his face so other track workers wouldn't recognize him.

"Do you think this is the picture the killer wanted to steal?" I asked. "It doesn't look good for Frank."

"Maybe, but I don't know how he saw me."

"We had the camera when we tried to enter the stables after the races, remember?"

"Yeah. Let's see if anything else stands out."

For the next hour, we pored over the pictures. We clicked on every single image, searching as if it contained the answer to the meaning of life. I paid special attention to every shot with the betting windows in the background, but if Frank placed a bet, he'd done it when Cal wasn't looking. We flagged a few other shots with Morgan or Frank in them for review later, but nothing else jumped out as obviously suspicious.

When we got to the end, Cal suggested a break before we started over. Although I'd eaten a large dinner at Kevin's house, Cal had stopped by the local bakery before picking me up and grabbed cupcakes for all four of us. Now he brought out a plate for us to share.

"What's Frank's motive?" Cal asked.

With the first bite, I felt better. Sugar always helped me think. "Frank and Morgan were betting on races, which is prohibited."

"Are you sure?"

"Pretty sure," I said. "I don't know the details. How did it work? Did they only bet on long odds? How did she guarantee that she'd win?"

"She can't," Cal said. "It's hard to imagine anyone would take such a big risk with such a small chance of reward, unless they were extremely confident. I guess she believed in her abilities."

"Or she had a lot of debt," I said, thinking of Florence's student loans. "Maybe they needed money badly enough to make any reward worth the risk. We don't know what Morgan's finances were like."

"You didn't find anything when you searched her dorm?"

"Only this." Pulling out my phone, I swiped to an image of one of the more bizarre messages. "I thought Morgan was setting up meetings with a lover, but now I'm sure it's related to the scheme."

"Let me see." Cal took my phone and peered closer. "You're right. If they always bet on Morgan, they'd only need the race number. It's a great system—without the background, these texts are meaningless."

"We need to confirm that Morgan ran in each of these races. Can you pull up last year's results online?"

"Brilliant!" Cal pulled me in for a quick kiss before sitting back at the computer. "Absolutely brilliant. What's the first one?"

Starting at the end, I peered at the dates on the screen. "September 4, fifth race."

Cal pulled up the race results quickly. "Morgan came in sixth riding a horse that was favored to win 26-1."

"Sixth? She didn't win?" It made no sense. Why set up an illegal betting scheme if you didn't make money? Morgan's horse had been a favorite. "What's the payout on those odds?"

"Just like it sounds. For every dollar bet, you'd get ten back. She'd need to put down a lot of money to make it worth losing her job, especially if they split the winnings."

"TJ thought the races were rigged. Did Morgan mess up?"

Cal shrugged. "Like I said, there are a ton of factors in any race. It's hard to ensure a win."

I sighed. "Let's find the next one. August 23, third race."

"Morgan came in fourth. Her horse was favored to win 23-1."

I shook my head. "I don't get it."

"I think I do," Cal said. "It's perfect when you think about it. Morgan isn't supposed to win."

I tilted my head like I hadn't heard him correctly. "Can you bet against a specific horse?"

"Sure you can. They couldn't do it often, or it would look suspicious. Check out the dates. It's sporadic. No jockey wins every time. Her losses blend in with the others. Unless you're looking for the pattern, you'd never see it."

"The partner wanted Morgan to throw her race on Sunday, and she refused," I said. "That's the final text."

"In your vision, you said Morgan was really pushing for the win, right?"

"Yeah. And after she won, she said, 'it's over.' Now I get it. She'd been told to lose on purpose, and she refused. She was out. Then her partner killed her."

"It makes sense," Cal said. "Morgan's mount was the favorite in the second race. Anyone who bet on her to lose could have gotten a big payout. Her partner must have been furious when she crossed the finish line."

"It's a great theory, but we can't prove it. Frank's not going to admit his involvement," I said.

"Maybe he won't have to," Cal said. "Morgan thought Bryce's car accident was deliberate. What if the collision wasn't to keep Bryce from racing, but a warning?"

I was out of my chair and halfway to the door before he finished his sentence. "We need to talk to Bryce again."

Cal and I rushed to his car, barely pausing to tell Rusty we were leaving.

"Do you think he'll talk to us?" Cal said after we got on the road. "Earlier, he didn't say a thing about illegal betting."

"Jacob works at the track. Bryce might have been afraid he'd tell," I said. "I wish we'd pushed harder."

We parked in the lot next to the dorms and walked over. I scanned the area to see if anyone might be watching us or Bryce's apartment. Nothing. Cal's fears made me paranoid.

When I called Bryce to request door access, no one responded. He had to be home, so he must not want visitors. Luckily, I had many ways to get in. I buzzed another unit.

After a moment, a female voice answered. "Hello?"

"Your food's here!" I said cheerfully. Most people opened the door for deliveries.

"Wrong apartment," she said.

The door remained firmly shut.

"Do we have to try that thirty times?" Cal said. "It might be easier to keep buzzing Bryce until he answers."

"No. I have another idea."

I took a deep breath and examined the keypad. While most of my visions came from strong emotions, we left psychic traces on everything we touched. When the same person used an item repeatedly, those impressions built up over time.

Closing my eyes, I pressed the zero button. Immediately, in my mind's eye, I saw a hand pushing in a code. Once I repeated the sequence, the door popped open.

Cal shook his head. "Even knowing about your abilities, it's amazing to see them in action."

"Just doing my job," I said.

Halfway to the elevator, I noticed a streak of something brownish-red on the wall. "What's that?"

"It looks like paint," Cal said. "Was this there before?"

"No, it was not."

The pit of my stomach tightened. The stain didn't look like paint to me. It looked like dried blood. I raced past the elevator and took the stairs two at a time to the second floor.

Upstairs, I noticed scuff marks on the wall extending from the elevator halfway down the hallway. "Those weren't there before, either."

"Someone moving out?" Cal asked. "It could be from furniture."

"Or it could be something else," I said grimly. "They start at Bryce's place."

The two of us rushed down the hall. When we arrived, I banged on the door. It swung open beneath my touch.

The pit in my stomach grew larger. "That's not a good sign."

"No, it's not." Cal pulled out his phone. "I'm calling 911."

"Hold on." I leaned into the room. "Hello? Bryce? Are you here?"

No response.

Cal was already talking to someone. "Marie says not to go in."

"Who?"

"The 911 operator."

"Bryce could be hurt. I have to check."

Ignoring Cal's protest, I stepped into the room. It didn't take long to investigate. With the door open, we could already see half of the tiny dorm. Two steps inside showed the rest.

The sheets on the empty bed were twisted. Pillows lay on the ground on opposite sides of the room. Inside the open closet door, several hangers appeared to have been knocked aside or torn down.

"Bryce?" I called again.

Nothing. My trepidation grew stronger.

Already knowing what I'd find, I hurried into the bathroom. Empty. I peeked behind the shower curtain, just in case, although I felt foolish. Finally, I had to acknowledge the truth.

Bryce was gone.

# CHAPTER TWENTY-TWO

WE WAITED in the hall for the police to arrive. Cal leaned against the wall, gazing at the threadbare carpet.

"Are you okay?"

He shook his head. Poor guy had never been this close to a crime scene. I leaned against the wall beside him and held his hand in silent support. We remained that way until the elevator dinged.

When Sheriff Matthews stepped into the hallway, I groaned inwardly. Every time I called for assistance, I prayed Doug would receive the message instead of his uncle.

"Aly Reynolds," he said with a smirk. "I should have known. What are you doing here?"

"An excellent question," Cal muttered. I glanced at him, but he ignored me.

"Cal's cousin is friends with Bryce," I said to the sheriff. "We were talking to him earlier. I came back to ask him something."

"You're not interfering with police work again, are you? I've told you to leave the investigating to the professionals." He turned to Cal. "Why are you encouraging her? One of these days, someone's going to get hurt."

Cal's face turned red. "Sorry, sir."

"Excuse me," I said loudly. "I'm a grown adult."

"You should be," Sheriff Matthews said to Cal. "Listen, I'm going to secure the crime scene. You two go home. Now. Scat."

He watched as we pushed the elevator button. Neither of us spoke until we were inside and the doors shut behind us.

"That's some thank you," I said. "I've half solved this case for him and he tells me to go away?"

"He's right."

The quiet words made my head snap up. "What?"

"He said investigating is dangerous, and he's right," Cal said. "We're chasing a *killer*. You saw that mess, all the blood. This is a job for the police. We should have stayed out of it."

"What? Why?" His statement was such a reversal, I thought I'd misheard him. We'd been working for days to crack this case. We found Morgan's killer, and he wanted to back off?

"Aly, think about it. Frank broke Bryce's legs, killed Morgan, then kidnapped Bryce. He's dangerous."

"I investigate dangerous stuff all the time. Why is this different? I thought you wanted to help Jacob."

"Not if helping gets you killed." He sighed, keeping his gaze focused on the numbers above the elevator door. We realized at the same time that we weren't moving. No one had pushed the button. "Normally, when you're working a case, I'm not beside you. I never realized how many risks you take."

"That's why I took self-defense classes," I said, hitting the number one so we could leave. "We came to ask Bryce a few questions. I'm not dumb enough to call Frank and accuse him of murder. Give me some credit."

"You're not dumb at all. That's what worries me," Cal said. "What happens when Frank realizes you're onto him?"

"Nothing, because he won't. The police are involved. Doug will be here soon, and we can tell him what we found. He'll complete the investigation. Sheriff Matthews can arrest the killer and take all the credit. We'll be completely safe, and justice will be served." I paused. "Well, mostly. Except for that last part. But I'm not helping for the glory."

Cal muttered something under his breath.

"What was that?"

He sighed. "I said, 'I wonder why I'm doing this at all.' I don't have investigative skills. I don't have psychic powers. I'm just the jerk who put his girlfriend in danger."

"Oh, no, none of that." I glared at him. "I make my own decisions. Jacob was in trouble, and I agreed to help. I have a unique skill set. Should we let him go to jail because of some misguided belief that you need to protect me?"

Cal sighed. "No, of course not. I'm sorry."

This conversation could have become a much bigger argument, but Cal meant well. The last couple of days had been difficult. He'd never seen all this murder stuff so close up before. Even when I got taken hostage last spring, Cal didn't know until after I'd been released. He missed the fear of the moment.

When I first found out about my powers, they scared me, too. Then I realized I could help people. At first, I didn't realize how dangerous investigating a murder could be. Cal was new to this. I should have eased him in.

Neither of us spoke as we exited the building. Everyone said couples should find an activity they enjoyed doing together, but investigating murders was not a fun date. Zero stars, did not recommend.

"What do we do now?" We were so close to figuring everything out. Giving up now nauseated me, but we couldn't catch Frank while arguing.

"I don't know." He sighed. "I'm scared, Aly. Frank killed Morgan. He broke into your car to leave a warning. When you ignored it, he kidnapped Bryce. I'm terrified something is going to happen to you. Or Jake or me. We should tell the police everything and walk away."

"You heard Sheriff Matthews," I said. "He couldn't have

been less interested in who I think killed Morgan. Tomorrow, we'll ask Jacob to confirm the identity of the Chiefs fan in the picture. You don't need to be part of this anymore."

"That's not necessary," he said quietly.

"I think it is," I whispered. "I'm sorry you got dragged into this with me."

"I'm not. Now I know what you're doing when you're out solving cases. You've made it sound like a fun adventure— like putting together pieces of a puzzle."

"That's how I see it."

"I get that. But your average jigsaw isn't fatal."

There was no need to respond. Yes, chasing murderers was dangerous. Under the wrong circumstances, crossing the street or going to a concert could be dangerous. Pointing that out wouldn't ease Cal's concerns.

Outside, I paused at the entrance to the parking lot, scanning the cars.

"What are you doing?" Cal asked.

"Looking for Doug."

"You think Shady Grove will send both their officers for something like this?"

"I think Sheriff Matthews hates late nights and will want Doug to process the scene. I'll text him."

Cal looked toward his car and back at me. His clenched jaw told me what he thought of my continued involvement. As badly as Cal wanted to get away from this investigation, he wouldn't leave me here alone at night. "You show Doug the evidence, then we're leaving. Got it?"

"Got it. Thanks for waiting with me."

He didn't answer.

When Doug arrived, I filled him in on everything Sheriff Matthews hadn't wanted to hear and showed him the pictures of Morgan's burner phone texts. He let out a low whistle. "This is great. Thanks. Now we can prove motive. Text me these pictures, okay?"

After forwarding everything, I said, "We've got pictures

from the track on Sunday, too. They're on Rusty's computer, but I can send a link to your work email so you have them officially. There's one of a track employee glaring at Morgan not long before she died. You should talk to him."

"Thanks," Doug said. "You're amazing. We should deputize you."

"Please don't encourage her," Cal muttered.

I shot him a pointed look. "I heard that."

Cal started to say something else, but Doug cleared his throat. "Anything else?"

"Oh! Yes, we found a betting ticket in the locker room. Which, now that I think about, you're going to tell me I should have left there because I destroyed the chain of custody."

"Do you have it on you?"

My face flamed. "I think it's in my car. But I could testify to what was on it!"

"What was on it?"

"I, um… numbers and stuff?" I sighed. "Sorry."

"Jake can do it," Cal said.

I nodded. "Yeah, he saw it, too. Doug, we're pretty sure there were more illegal bets. Does the track keep records of that stuff?"

"They must," he said.

"They do," Cal said. "I don't know how long they're kept, but the records exist."

"Can we cross-reference the races Morgan threw with the bets against her?" I asked. One ticket didn't prove anything, especially without knowing who'd bought it. If we got half a dozen, though, that could pull the case together.

"Depends on whether the track keeps those records," Doug said. "If so, we can pull every bet against Morgan's horse in each race and cross-reference."

"It would take weeks," Cal said. "Betting against horses is pretty common. Not to mention, the bets could have been placed online or using cash."

I sighed. "It's hopeless."

"Don't give up yet," Doug said. "We're examining every angle."

"What now?" I asked.

"Go home. Take the rest of the night off. Thanks for everything."

Cal strode to the car, tight-lipped. When we got in, he said, "I can't believe it. We hand them the whole case, and he blows us off. Doesn't he understand what you're risking to help?"

"He does," I said. "And so do I, in case you've forgotten. This isn't about pinning the case on anyone. Doug wants to arrest the right guy, and so do I."

"Of course you're defending him." He pulled out of the parking spot, and I gazed out the window.

We couldn't communicate when this upset. I wasn't sure what we were arguing about, anyway. We were here because Cal wanted me to save Jacob! How was I going to clear his name without finding the real killer? Investigating a murder meant taking some risks. During my last case, I got kidnapped and almost set on fire. Cal didn't mind asking me to help his cousin after that. What changed?

With both of us fuming, the drive home lasted an eternity. When Cal dropped me off, he kissed me gently. "I'm sorry about tonight."

Although I understood how much walking into a crime scene shook him, I worried about his reaction. My powers were a big part of my identity. Cal had glimpsed this part of my life, and he didn't like it. Could he accept who I was before our differences ripped us apart?

# CHAPTER TWENTY-THREE

THE NEXT MORNING, Olive and I met at Missing Pieces to exercise my powers before my shift. As badly as I wanted to race to the track and interrogate Frank until he confessed the truth, Doug had said they had everything under control. I trusted Doug.

Rusty had read about Penny's murder and was developing his own theories. For me to contribute in any meaningful way, I needed to hone my powers. The store didn't open until ten, so Olive agreed to meet me at eight.

Considering how many cases I'd solved while looking into Katrina's murder, I'd thought it would be easier to juggle two investigations. However, I'd known the facts of Katrina's case before discovering my powers. Keeping the details of Penny's and Morgan's deaths straight in my mind was exhausting.

In the little sleep I'd gotten, I dreamed of Tripp placing bets at a frat party with two broken legs using puka shells as currency. I couldn't wait until Doug arrested Frank so I could give Penny's case my full attention.

When I arrived, I took Tripp's necklace from where it had been tucked away. We knew the piece belonged to him and he was the person in my vision. Focusing on the necklace might help me isolate Tripp's energy, then identify the same energy elsewhere.

Yeah, I didn't really understand Olive's explanation, either. But I had to try. Imagine being able to touch a murder weapon and know who had wielded it. Armed with that information, I could send anonymous tips to the police and tell them exactly which suspect to focus on.

Developing this ability could clear Jacob's name, get Tripp released from prison, and solve dozens of cold cases. Not to mention new ones. My ability to help people would expand exponentially. If it worked.

Unfortunately, that remained a big "if."

When I arrived, I handed Olive a drink from the coffee shop next door. My boss liked living on the edge; she always told Julie to "surprise her." The last time I asked, Julie created something with peppermint, pumpkin spice, and marshmallow, so I'd stopped asking what was in the cup. Olive accepted it with a smile, then took a sip. "Ah, delightful. Just a hint of anise and coconut."

I shuddered and sipped my drink, grateful that it tasted like espresso, milk, and vanilla, as usual.

"You look exhausted," she said.

"Thanks." I grimaced at her. "Everyone loves to hear they look awful."

"Stop. You know what I mean. Is everything okay?"

"I was up late last night." I gave her an abbreviated version.

"You've been busy," she said when I finished. "Are you sure you want to jump into practice this morning?"

"Yeah. Doug expects to arrest Frank today. All I can do is hope for the best," I said. "Besides, I made a commitment to Lucy and Rusty. Did you find out anything about one object holding multiple memories?"

Although Olive and I both knew witches on the council that helped keep the magic community under control (and secret!), she was more comfortable reaching out to them for assistance. To me, calling Lilia for supernatural advice was as daunting as asking Taylor Swift for singing lessons.

"Lilia said if the emotions tied to the memories were strong enough, it could happen. Penny's death would certainly cause Tripp to anguish over their final interactions. The necklace might carry different events from that same night."

"Any other possibilities?"

"The choppiness could be because of the alcohol. Just like someone who drank too much might feel fuzzy the next morning," Olive said. "Lilia offered to examine the necklace."

I hesitated. "Let's keep using it for our tests."

"Think about it. You can always change your mind."

Once again, we started with tea and meditation. When I was ready, I put on Tripp's necklace and watched the party scenes. This time, I focused my energy on the feelings rather than the physical experience. His emotions came through clearly, but they didn't feel unique to him.

After an hour, I didn't feel any differently. Maybe it couldn't be done. With a heavy sigh, I drained my latte.

"You're working hard," Olive said. "Take a break. We'll try again."

A break didn't get me any closer to the truth. Maybe I could instead get information from the closest thing I had to an eyewitness. Other than Tripp. "You were at the party, right?"

"Yes, but I left long before anything happened. Did you see me?"

"I wasn't sure at first, but I think so. When Tripp first entered the room, you were in the corner talking to Mayor Banister. Well, she wasn't the mayor back then, I guess."

"I don't remember seeing Tripp, but Beth has a way of taking up all your attention. Probably why she's always been popular."

"Were you two friends?"

"We got along most of the time." Olive paused. "I'm not

going to ask Beth what she remembers, if that's what you're getting at."

I shook my head. "No, I got her statements from the newspaper. What were you talking about at the party?"

"Nothing, really. She'd won a student service award earlier that day. She brought it to the party and showed it off, talking about how hard she'd worked and how much she deserved it."

"The mayor used to do actual work?" Olive snorted, so I said, "Sorry. What was the award for?"

"Beth was an organizer, even back then. Constantly getting people to do things. She can be very charismatic." Olive paused, lost in the memory. "I don't remember the details. Some project she'd worked on with Penny and their other friend, Tricia. All I remember is thinking I needed a drink if she kept going on about herself."

"I didn't realize you knew them so well."

"It's a small town." She smiled. "I wouldn't say we were besties, but Beth, Tricia, and I went to high school together. With so few students, when one person blinked, the rest of the class knew."

I closed my eyes, picturing the scene. "There's also this guy in my vision, walking around with some kind of sword. I don't remember his name, but did they look at a weird sword guy?"

"Of course. Richard was a member of the fencing team. He carried his épée everywhere. He and Tripp worked at the Golf Club together during the summers. The police didn't find any blood on his blade. They couldn't test for DNA back then."

I filed that information away. "Did Richard have any reason to kill Penny?"

"Not that I'm aware of."

Later, I wanted to dig deeper into Richard and the guy Penny had been flirting with. Now, it was time to work on my powers. After rewatching the party scenes, I removed the necklace.

Since weddings and births were some of the events most closely tied to strong emotions, I tried on a platinum band that turned out to be Lucy's wedding ring. It treated me to a lovely scene from the day Lucy married Tripp's father; however, I only knew it was Lucy's from the fact that people kept toasting "To Lucy and Preston, Jr.!" They looked so happy, it hurt to think about the pain to follow.

The other items followed the same pattern. A few gave me visions, some didn't, but nothing let me identify the individual behind the memory.

"Have we considered the possibility that this isn't something I can accomplish?" I asked when it was time to open the store.

"Don't give up. I'm going to the magic shop to get some herbs," Olive said. "Maybe some stronger incense."

"Are you trying to get me high?"

She chuckled. "No. I'll ask Amira if she has any other ideas."

"Thanks for trying," I said.

The magic store, run by a friend of ours, was about half a block down Main Street. While I waited for Olive to return, I opened the blinds over the front windows, got the cash drawer from the safe to add to the register, then walked around the store, mentally reviewing my opening checklist.

Right after Olive left, the bell over the front door jingled. "Did you forget something?"

Silence.

From my vantage point, I couldn't see the front doors, so I tried again. "Olive?"

"It's me."

Jacob stood in the middle of the front room, bent over and panting like he'd won the Kentucky Derby. As the horse.

I went to him. "Are you okay?"

He tried to stand upright, revealing a black eye and bloodied lip. He took two steps toward me, then collapsed against the patio table set near the register. "So... glad... here!"

I raced to his side. "What's wrong?"

"Cal." Jacob doubled over, breathing heavily. "Gone."

"Hold on. What happened? Where's Cal?"

"They took him," he panted.

"Who? Why?"

His word punched me in the gut. "Killers.... Morgan. They got Cal."

# CHAPTER TWENTY-FOUR

THIS COULDN'T BE HAPPENING. I must not have heard Jacob correctly. "Frank took Cal? Why?"

When Jacob opened his mouth, no words came out. I raced to the back and filled a glass of water, sloshing half of it on myself and the floor while carrying it back. He gulped it down. By the time he'd finished, his breathing had returned to almost normal.

"Cal and I were at his place. Two guys burst in, both wearing masks. One of them was big, like Frank. How did you know it was him?"

"The sweatshirt. I'll explain later. Go on."

Jacob continued, "It happened fast. The smaller one put a bag over Cal's head. I lunged toward him, and the big guy punched me. I went down. When I tried to get up, one of them kicked me. I passed out. When I came to, everyone was gone."

I struggled to wrap my head around his story. "That doesn't make sense. Why would Frank want Cal?"

"They kept asking about his camera," Jacob said miserably. "This is my fault. I told everyone we'd find the killer, and they took Cal."

Although I personally agreed, this wasn't the time to point

fingers. If we got my boyfriend back safely, Jacob would get an earful about discretion.

I couldn't believe I'd been so stupid.

We knew the killers wanted the camera. We'd even found the photographs! After talking to Doug, I'd stupidly forgotten owning the camera still put Cal in danger.

The room spun.

No. Save Cal now. Panic later.

"We need to call the police," I said.

"No!" The fear in his voice made me freeze. "Can't. Hold on. When I woke up, I found a note. It said, 'Come to 42 Spring Street. Bring the camera by noon. Tell no one or he dies. If you're late, he dies.'"

My body sagged against the counter.

Jacob caught me. "It'll be okay. We can save him. We just need the camera. I looked, but it wasn't in Cal's apartment. Do you know where it is?"

"Yeah." In theory. My thoughts swirled too quickly to grab onto any. I barely remembered my own name, much less where Cal had left his camera. We'd been going through the pictures before leaving for Bryce's—did we take it?

Reciting the periodic table cleared my head, but there wasn't time. I'd do it in the car. I was halfway to the back to grab my keys before remembering I'd walked to work that morning. My car was still at the mechanic; it wouldn't be ready until this afternoon at the earliest.

"Can you drive?"

"No problem."

We raced to his car, with me barely pausing to flip the sign on the front door to "Closed" on my way out. I'd text Olive from the car once we were on our way.

When Cal and I had arrived at the stables on Sunday, both security guards saw me holding the camera. Frank must have seen Cal taking pictures while he stood in line. What I didn't understand was why my boyfriend stood out more in his mind than anyone else.

"This doesn't make sense," I said, buckling my seatbelt. "Lots of people had cameras. Why Cal?"

"Lots of people brought cameras, but how many were at the stables before and after Morgan died?"

It hadn't occurred to me that the killer might be hanging around the stables when Cal and I returned, but of course, if it was Frank, we'd talked to him.

Or maybe the killer knew Cal took pictures because someone told his friends we had photos.

No. That kind of finger-pointing wasn't helpful.

We fell silent. As we drove away from Missing Pieces, I remembered Cal and I leaving his camera at my place in our rush to get to Bryce's dorm. When Cal dropped me off later, he didn't come inside to get it. He'd barely said goodbye.

At the time, I'd been sad, but now I was grateful. If Cal had taken the camera home, the guy who kidnapped him might've killed him on the spot.

"I can't believe this," I said. "The camera's at my place."

I gave him my address, and he repeated it into his GPS. "Did you review the pictures? What did you see?"

"A reporter went to meet a source about a gambling scheme at the racetrack. The source never showed up, but we found a picture of Morgan standing nearby. We thought her accomplice saw her and realized she planned to expose him. But we didn't get anything that would stand up in court. A guy who might have been Frank standing in the crowd, but it could have been one of a million football fans."

Jacob gave me a sharp look. "You saw Frank?"

"We think so. His face was covered, but it looked like the sweatshirt from the locker room. I was going to ask you to confirm it after work." I sighed. "We should've confronted Frank with the pictures last night and forced him to confess."

"Don't beat yourself up. You couldn't have known. Me, on the other hand…" He sighed. "I'm sorry you got caught up in this. If I hadn't argued with Morgan, no one would have suspected me. Then you and Cal would be safe."

Jacob's voice cracked. I shot him a sideways glance. He gripped the steering wheel with white knuckles, eyes focused on the road like it might disappear.

"Don't blame yourself," I said. "No one made me get involved."

Poor guy. I'd known this whole thing affected him, obviously, but the shadows under his eyes spoke volumes. He'd lost weight, too. In this past week, Jacob had found a coworker's body, got accused of murder, watched his favorite cousin get kidnapped, and got punched in the head.

I had to do something. Maybe I could induce a vision of the kidnapper writing that note to find the second killer's identity. They might have said something after Jacob got knocked out, or maybe I could get a feel for the person's identity if we'd met at the track.

Just because my tests hadn't worked earlier didn't mean it was never possible. A memory from less than an hour ago was fresher than memories in boxes delivered to Missing Pieces in March.

"Do you have the note?" I asked.

"Uh, yeah? Why?"

"We're rushing into a hostage situation. I want to see what the note can tell me."

"Are you into that handwriting analysis mumbo jumbo? You know, that's not a science. It's worse than fortune-telling."

"Yeah." I forced a laugh. "You're right. It's dumb. But I'd feel better."

With a shrug, Jacob reached into his pocket and pulled out the note.

The paper itself wasn't interesting. It appeared to be an ordinary sheet from a printer, now crumpled. It could've been taken from Cal's apartment when they grabbed him, but it also could have come from literally any business or the public computers at the library.

The letters were big and dark, written in all caps, probably using a black Sharpie. Cal had those at his house, which told me nothing. So did a lot of people.

"Did they have this note when they walked in?" I asked.

He shrugged. "I didn't see it until I woke up. I figured they wrote it on the way out."

Hopefully they'd been flustered, because this would work better if the note writer experienced strong emotions. I took a deep breath and closed my eyes, reaching for my powers. With my right hand, I traced the blocky black letters as if writing them myself.

*When I opened my eyes, I was in Cal's apartment. My left hand now held a Sharpie, hovering above the paper.*

*"Come on, we don't have all day," a male voice growled.*

*"I'm thinking," I replied.*

The voice nearly knocked me out of the vision, but I held on. The first voice sounded familiar. It wasn't Frank. The voice belonged to Robert. Even only speaking with them a couple of times, I recognized it instantly. They didn't sound alike.

But the second kidnapper, the person who held the pen—I knew that voice very well. After working so hard all morning, I recognized the essence of the note writer, too. My heart sank, and I struggled to maintain my grip on the vision.

*Cal lay on the floor of his apartment, slumped on one side. He was unconscious, but his chest rose and fell.*

*"Hurry up and write the note while I get this guy outside."* Definitely Robert. How had we gotten that wrong?

*"I've got it."*

*"This better work," Robert said.*

*"It'll work," his accomplice said.*

*"Are you sure the girl has the camera?" Robert yanked his mask off and rubbed his face with both hands.*

*"Positive. Now hit me. Not too hard."*

*"Of course not." He smiled thinly. "Just because this whole thing is your fault, why would I hit you hard?"*

*"Hey, man. I didn't want—" A meaty white fist came toward*

I gasped. When my world returned to normal, my hands shook.

"Are you okay?"

"Y-yeah." I forced myself to remain under control. "It just, I guess it feels more real now. The urgency. I, um, I hope we get there in time to save him."

"Don't worry," Jacob said. "We'll make it."

His words gave me zero relief. Not after that vision.

The person writing the note was left-handed. The voice unmistakably belonged to Jacob. I wanted to believe Robert forced him to write it, but Jacob told Robert to hit him before he left. He wanted it to look like he'd been a victim.

Robert's words jumped out at me. "Your fault." Was he talking to the person who killed Morgan? Closing my eyes, I pulled up the memory of my vision from Wind Walker's stall. Then I compared every detail to this one. A week ago, I wouldn't have noticed, but I'd been studying visions all week. Both memories felt the same. Part of it was the anger, but it was the essence of the person whose mind I'd inhabited. It was almost like a brain signature.

A jury would never buy it, but I knew the truth.

The person who killed Morgan wrote the note. The person writing the note used their left hand. Jacob was left-handed. Cal mentioned it back when Jacob talked about breaking his right arm as a kid.

When Robert said it was Jacob's fault he needed to kidnap Cal, he didn't mean because Jacob invited us to the track and we happened to take an incriminating photograph. He'd meant that Jacob had created this entire problem by killing Morgan.

The police had been right all along.

# CHAPTER TWENTY-FIVE

MY HEART POUNDED in my ears. This had to be a mistake. Jacob killed Morgan. Jacob, the man currently sitting beside me in the car. The guy taking me to the killers pretending we were going to rescue Cal. No! No way.

I refused to believe it. Unfortunately, visions didn't lie.

Okay, stay calm. The most important thing was that Jacob didn't realize I was onto him.

Element one was hydrogen. Element two was helium. Element three was lithium. Jacob was a killer.

Mentally, I called myself ten kinds of idiot. Cal and I had been so close to this case, we never stopped to consider whether Morgan had been right. Jacob caused Bryce's car accident as a warning after Morgan quit the scheme. When she refused to throw the second race, making them lose their wager, Jacob killed her.

Desperate to control my rising panic, I studied the landscape beyond the window. There must be a safe place to jump out of the car. My fist clenched around the note.

Then I deflated. If I jumped out of the car and ran, Robert would kill Cal. Even if I called Doug immediately, he'd never get there in time. I needed stay calm so Jacob kept thinking I believed him.

"Anything interesting in that note?" Jacob asked casually.

I struggled to keep my tone light. "Florence didn't write it. The handwriting is too good. Doctors have terrible writing."

"Heh. Yeah. You're smart, like Cal said."

"Fat lot of good it did us. Cal's been kidnapped and we're racing off to meet with someone who probably plans to kill us."

"You don't know that," Jacob said. His hands twisted on the wheel. "Cal didn't back up his pictures on the cloud, did he? Or show them to anyone besides you?"

"Um, no," I said. "No copies."

"You sure? Most cameras connect to Wi-Fi."

"Cal hadn't set it up yet," I lied. "The camera's new. We should call the police and give them the address. They can meet us there."

Jacob tapped the note where it lay on the console between us. "No cops. It's an easy trade. The camera for Cal."

"Do you know the address? How far is it?"

"From your house? Probably twenty minutes."

We were running out of time. While I didn't think Robert would hurt Cal before getting his hands on the camera, I wasn't prepared to stake my boyfriend's life on it.

When we arrived at Rusty and Doug's place, Jacob looked around as he shifted into park, leaving the engine running.

"Is the cop here now?"

"Probably not, but I have two roommates," I said. "Rusty sometimes works from home."

He nodded. "Play it cool. If anything goes wrong, I don't want to think about what will happen to Cal."

"I'll do my best," I said. "But if we rush in and out without talking to Rusty, he'll know something's wrong. He's my best friend."

"We've got a few extra minutes. Be cool. If you make a wrong move, Cal will die."

*Because of you.* My dark thoughts swirled. Now that we'd stopped, I wanted to lunge at him and scratch his eyes out.

But if I did that, he'd call his friends. If we didn't show up, they'd kill Cal. If someone other than Jacob's car pulled up to the building, they'd kill Cal. I couldn't take that risk.

Jacob and I would go together to take Robert the camera as planned. It was the only way to protect Cal. I just needed to warn Rusty without Jacob knowing.

Good thing I'd done the spring play after all. Summoning every bit of my acting ability, I took a deep breath and threw my head back. "We can do this. For Cal."

When we entered the condo, Rusty sat at his computer in the dining room. "What are you doing home? I thought you were working all day."

The concern on his face almost broke me. As much as I wanted to blurt out the truth, I couldn't endanger Cal. Worse, Rusty would also become a target if I dragged him into this. I needed to stay calm, stick to the plan, and keep him safe.

"Yeah, sorry. I took an early lunch. This is Jacob, Cal's cousin. Cal needs his camera before my shift ends, so Jacob's going to take it to him. We'll get out of your way in a minute." When our eyes met, I held Rusty's gaze, trying desperately to convey the severity of the situation.

The camera sat where we'd left it on the dining room table. With shaking hands, I packed it up. Rusty watched my every move.

After I zipped up the bag, I flung the strap over my shoulder and asked, "You still having dinner with Doug's family tonight?"

Since he wasn't a local, Jacob wouldn't know that Doug's uncle was our sheriff. I didn't want him to realize I was asking Rusty for help.

The probability of me and Cal being released unharmed approached zero. Assuming Cal was even still alive. Letting Rusty know something was up could save our lives without endangering my friend.

"Yeah, definitely," Rusty said. "Uncle Tim makes a mean chicken."

Message received. Hopefully. It was my only chance. "Bring me some leftovers?"

"Ha! There won't be any leftovers."

When Jacob opened the front door, Rusty said, "Hold on. You forgot the spare battery pack."

As he passed me the item, Rusty squeezed my hand. I peered into his concerned blue eyes, and he widened his gaze in a silent question. My eyes shifted back and forth in an almost imperceptible 'no.' *No, everything is not okay.*

"Thanks!" I said brightly. "I'll see you after dinner. Tell Tim I said hi. Wish I could be there."

"He'll be devastated."

As we walked out the door, I prayed Rusty would save me and Cal. It was our only chance.

# CHAPTER TWENTY-SIX

WHEN JACOB and I got back into his car, I checked the time. We'd been inside longer than I'd wanted. Although I now knew the deadline was a lie to trick me into bringing the camera to the warehouse, I held my breath while buckling my seatbelt.

"Please hurry," I begged Jacob. "We need to get there in time. You can't let anything happen to Cal!"

Was I laying it on a little thick? Sure, but the rising hysteria was real. He needed to believe my concern was for Cal and not because I'd figured out the truth.

"I'm on it. I'm a jockey, remember? We were made for speed." He smiled in a manner that would have reassured me if I didn't know the truth.

How could he do this to us? Sure, I was practically a stranger, but Cal was family.

Okay, Aly. Make a plan now, be furious later.

Every instinct screamed at me to leap out of the car, despite getting in voluntarily. At least Rusty was safe.

"Why do you keep looking out the window?" he asked.

"Um, so we can tell the police how to find the bad guys after we save Cal."

"We have the address."

I winced. "Right. We should give it to them. Later."

The locks clicked shut. "You're not going anywhere, Aly."

"What are you talking about?"

"Come on," he said. "I don't know how you recognized my writing, but it's clear you did. You've been weird ever since reading the note. Let's drop the pretense."

"Don't do this," I said desperately. "I don't know anything, but Rusty saw us together. You'll be in trouble if I never go home."

"After we're done, I'll take care of Rusty. Don't worry about that."

Panic rose in my throat. "How can you be so cavalier about the loss of human life?"

"Look, it's nothing personal. I'm looking out for myself," he said. "The three of us had a good thing before Morgan told her boyfriend. Bryce convinced her to quit. Said if she didn't, he'd get us banned from the track."

With great effort, I avoided pointing out that the people running a gambling ring and rigging horse races deserved to be thrown out of the sport forever.

"What did you do to Bryce?"

"What are you talking about?" he asked.

"Last night, Cal and I went to see him. His place was trashed, and he was gone."

"Huh," Jacob said. "I'll have to ask Robert."

"I don't understand," I said. "Why would you risk cheating? You have a promising career as a jockey."

"Jockeys don't make much at first. I needed to supplement. Last summer, Morgan approached me with this scheme. We were friends. Seemed like a great way to earn extra money without hurting anyone."

"Except the owners who don't get paid because their horse lost and the track paying out bets they shouldn't."

He snorted. "You want me to feel bad for the track owners? They make more every year than we'll earn in a lifetime."

"Okay, I get it," I said. "I'm broke, too, remember? What went wrong?"

"Bryce convinced Morgan to walk away. Robert thought if we gave her a warning, she'd stay in. She was right, you know. The collision wasn't an accident."

"It was you." Bewildered, I looked around the vehicle. "How? This car doesn't have a scratch on it."

"I didn't use my own car." His voice dripped with scorn. "Morgan became more determined to separate herself from our operation. When Robert saw her approach that reporter, he guessed her plan. She had to go. Unfortunately, you and Cal got a picture of all of them." He shook his head. "I still can't believe you realized it was me. Robert said I shouldn't let you try to solve the case, but I figured at best, you'd chase a few wild theories."

"Like you suggesting Morgan was having an affair with your gay boss?"

He chuckled. "That was fun."

"What about Frank's sweatshirt? Did you lie about that, too?"

"Nah. Robert borrowed it so no one would recognize him. Smart, huh?"

"Yeah, what a Rhodes scholar," I said bitterly.

"For what it's worth, I'm sorry you got wrapped up in this. You seem okay. I don't want to kill you."

"Me? Forget about me," I said. "How could you do this to Cal? Your favorite cousin? He's your best friend!"

"Is he?" Jacob laughed hollowly. "The guy who calls me Jake, knowing I hate it. Who caused me to get stitches because he didn't bother to pick up after himself. That entire summer, my mom wouldn't let me near a horse. I was miserable, stuck inside while she watched recorded episodes of *As the Hospital Guides Our Lives* over and over. Everyone else played outside. I was limping for six months! I can still hear the other kids laughing."

"That was twenty years ago!" I said desperately. "Cal didn't leave the hoof pick out on purpose."

"So he says. But come on. He's a smart guy. He had to know."

"Smart people do stupid things," I said. Like investigating murders with the killer by their side. "Last week, I walked into a vending machine."

He shook his head. "It's too late. I'm not going to jail."

"I won't tell anyone!" I'd have said anything to buy time. "Neither will Cal, I swear. The police will find Morgan's killer."

"It's too late. If I don't kill you, Robert will get all three of us."

"Call the police! Blame the whole thing on him. He rigged the security cameras, right? He placed the bet. He's all kinds of guilty. You can offer to testify in exchange for immunity."

"It'll never work. They'd lock us both up for conspiracy and murder."

I crossed my arms protectively across my chest. "You must have been cracking up when I went into Wind Walker's stall."

"Oh, yeah. We laughed so hard, we missed you going in and out."

Score one for Katrina's magical sunglasses.

"This is a joke to you," I said bitterly.

"It's not a joke, just a problem to be resolved. What gave me away?"

This wasn't the time to admit that my psychic powers told me the left-handed note writer had the same brain essence as the murderer.

"Cal mentioned when we met that you were left-handed. The letters on the note were tilted like a leftie wrote them." Was that a thing? I'd never studied handwriting analysis. Hopefully, neither had Jacob. "Robert disabled the cameras, right?"

"Smart girl," he said. "Yeah. He pulled the plug, then stayed with Frank to give himself an alibi and stand lookout.

We didn't want anyone to find Morgan until I got on the track."

The casual way he mentioned plotting murder terrified me even more. He hadn't gotten angry and hit Morgan in the heat of the moment. It hadn't been a bizarre accident that he'd covered up out of fear.

He'd intended to kill her, probably from the minute she confronted him. He kidnapped his own cousin. He planned to kill me, too.

I needed him to keep talking until I figured out how to save Cal.

"There's something I don't understand," I said.

He actually lifted his foot off the gas to look at me. "What?"

"Why did you ask for my help? You could have hired a lawyer or sat back and hoped the police botched the investigation."

"I didn't want your help!" He threw his hands up. "Stupid, meddling Cal insisted! He wouldn't shut up about you. 'Aly's so smart, Aly's so great, she'll fix everything!'"

In any other context, hearing those words would have warmed my heart. "You could have said no."

"I tried! He called my mom," Jacob said. "Besides, I never expected you to figure it out. I thought we could poke around, question people, point you in the wrong direction— you should have gotten frustrated and quit."

"I'm quite persistent," I said. "It's one of my finer qualities."

The car slowed. Jacob pulled into a lot behind a small, deserted-looking warehouse. I'd driven by this building a dozen times. According to signs, it was slated for destruction. Removing abandoned buildings seemed to be part of the mayor's re-election campaign, but since I wouldn't vote for her if they paid me, I didn't listen to her ads.

Jacob said, "We're going to get out of the car slowly. You're going to walk with me. Bring the camera."

"Why would I do that?"

"Because this doesn't have to hurt, but it can."

My mind raced. I'd come here to save Cal, but I couldn't walk into the warehouse at Jacob's side. I'd seen enough crime shows to know I'd never come out. Once I neutralized him, I'd rescue Cal.

When I didn't answer, Jacob got out of the driver's side and slammed the door. A moment later, the door beside me flew open.

"Come on. We've stalled long enough." He yanked me out of the car and dragged me toward the building.

Desperately, I grasped for more questions, anything to slow him down enough to give me an opening. "You broke into my car, too, right? What did you do with my backpack?"

"Chucked it in the dumpster once I realized it didn't have the camera."

"You know that wasn't my dress, right? I was supposed to give it back."

"Really? Well, now I feel terrible!"

"Your sarcasm is not appreciated," I said.

"Neither is your yapping."

Come on, Rusty. Where was he? Did I imagine him picking up my signals? I'd been sure he'd jump in his car and follow. I hadn't seen a single vehicle on the way here, though, and the area around the warehouse was silent.

Cal and I were running out of time.

"Who else is in on this? Did TJ help?"

"Keep moving." Jacob pushed me along.

"I lied before," I said desperately. "There is another copy of the pictures."

"Yeah?" He regarded me skeptically. I met his gaze steadily. After a moment, he shrugged. "That's okay. Eventually, you'll tell us where."

It was now or never. A million things could have held Rusty up, including him thinking something got in my eye when I signaled him. I refused to die waiting for a savior.

I stumbled on a crack in the pavement, falling into Jacob. He reached to steady me, but I jammed my elbow into his stomach. He grunted. Before he recovered, I flung my head back, slamming my skull into his nose. Jacob howled but kept hold of me. I stomped onto his instep, spun around, and kneed him in the crotch with all my strength. Then I grabbed his left arm and twisted it behind his back, slamming him into the wall.

"Ow! What the hell is wrong with you?"

"Me? You're trying to kill me," I said, pulling a gun from the waistband of his pants. "Should I lie down and take it?"

"Don't be a fool. You're a tiny woman."

"A tiny woman who incapacitated you." I snorted.

The gun went into an overgrown field beside the lot. I didn't know how to use it. Those weeds came up to my waist, and with all the summer storms, the whole area would be a muddy mess. If he got away from me, he'd be looking for a long time.

"You don't know what you're doing. If I yell, three guys will come out here. They might kill Cal first. I'm giving you one last chance to cooperate." He struggled against me, but I held firm. His phone poked out of a pocket, so I took it. It might hold important evidence, but it also went into the field.

"Let me make sure I understand," I spoke slowly, hoping he couldn't tell how my heart threatened to pound out of my chest. "You're offering me the stellar opportunity to release you so your friends can kill me and my boyfriend sooner?"

"Better than a slow death," he said.

"I've got a counter-offer," a voice said. "Ms. Reynolds, let go of Mr. Brunner and back up. Jacob, put your hands up."

I hardly dared take my eyes off Jacob, but a shift of my eyes revealed a police officer rounding the right corner of the building, about ten feet away. I put my hands up and slowly backed away from Jacob. Since I knew both the police officers in Shady Grove, I eyed this newcomer warily. Then he turned, and I recognized Detective Pratt, a homicide detective in Willow Falls.

Detective Pratt cuffed Jacob. "You are under arrest for murder, assault with a deadly weapon, and kidnapping. You have the right to remain silent."

"Cal is trapped inside the warehouse," I said. "There's a big guy in there with him. The security guard from the track."

"Don't worry. The sheriff is going in the front."

"Jacob said there are three of them!"

"Thanks," Tim said as he cuffed Jacob and continued his Miranda rights. "We'll be careful."

"Ay!" Doug and Rusty stepped around the left side of the building.

I raced to them. "They've got Cal. They're going to kill him. We have to get in there."

"No one is going to hurt him," Doug assured me. "Detective Pratt has everything under control."

"It's three on one!"

"No, it's not," Detective Pratt said. He had put Jacob into the police car and returned. "There's only one man inside with your boyfriend."

"Jacob lied about his accomplices?" I didn't know why that surprised me. He'd lied about a lot of things.

"Aly, I'm so sorry," Doug said. "Last night, I should have told you we had almost enough evidence to arrest Jacob. Uncle was worried Cal would tip him off, so I pretended we didn't suspect him."

"You knew?" That was why Sheriff Matthews didn't care about my theory of the case. He'd already figured it out.

"Not a hundred percent. We'd found Morgan's phone, but your information pulled it all together. Believe me, if I'd had the slightest idea you and Cal might be in danger..." His voice cracked. "Saratoga PD took an arrest warrant to Jacob's mom's house last night, and he wasn't there. I should have warned you then."

"Don't beat yourself up," I said. "You couldn't have known he'd go after us."

The back door to the warehouse opened, and Sheriff Matthews ushered Robert outside, hands cuffed behind his back.

Behind him came a police officer I'd never seen before, supporting Cal with an arm wrapped around his waist. She was at least a foot shorter than Cal, but he leaned on her heavily. The two of them trudged forward.

I resisted the urge to tackle my boyfriend and check him for injuries. "Is Cal okay? Why can't he walk?"

When he heard my voice, Cal looked up. He sported two black eyes, a split lip, and a bruise covered half his face. Still, he looked like the greatest thing I'd ever seen. He attempted to smile, then winced when the movement split his lip.

The policewoman stopped when she and Cal stood a couple of feet away. "I'm Officer Santiago. I'm going to be transferring to Shady Grove from the Saratoga PD. Does this guy belong to one of you?"

"Me!" I said. "He's mine. Cal, are you okay?"

"Yeah, I think so."

"He's a little banged up, but thanks to you, we arrived before they did any permanent damage," she said. "Cal, there's an ambulance out front to examine you before we take your statement. I need to go back inside."

I helped Cal limp to the paramedics. Even knowing they'd take care of him, I had trouble letting go. Cal squeezed my hand as if he understood. "I'm so glad to see you. I knew you'd figure everything out."

"I was wrong about the thing that mattered the most," I said miserably. "I put you in danger."

"No, I put myself in danger," he said. "I shouldn't have insisted Jake couldn't be involved. He's not who I thought."

"You couldn't have known Robert and Jacob conspired to kill Morgan." A thought hit me. "Was Bryce in there? Did anyone mention him?"

Cal nodded, wincing at the movement. "He's banged up but seemed okay."

A sigh of relief escaped me. "Poor guy. I'm sorry we didn't figure everything out sooner. Both of you would have been safe if I'd read the clues better."

"What are you talking about? I'm the one who asked you to work with a killer. You saved me!" Cal said. "How did you save me?"

I beckoned to my best friend, who stood a few feet away. "Not me, it was Rusty. All I did was get taken hostage."

"Lies. You saved yourself," Rusty said. "Cal, you should have seen her. She was brilliant. Making coded statements, keeping calm, disarming Jacob. That was all her. I just handed her a tracking device and followed with a cadre of police officers."

Cal bit his lip and nodded, looking a bit green. "Great thinking."

"I *knew* it!" I said. "Cal didn't have a spare battery pack at our place."

He shrugged. "You clearly didn't want Jacob to understand something was wrong."

"Good thinking." I hugged him. "Thank you for knowing exactly what I needed."

# EPILOGUE

THE NEXT MORNING, despite everything, I went to work as usual. Some people thought it weird, but since my power stemmed from antiques, being at the store settled me. After having my boyfriend kidnapped and almost being taken hostage, there was nowhere I'd rather be.

As soon as I flipped the sign to "Open," a familiar face appeared in the doorway. I yanked it open. "TJ! What are you doing here?"

"Can I come in?" He held up a copy of the *Shady Grove Sentinel.* "Brought you a present."

Surprised, I took it. An image showed Robert and Jacob being taken into the police station in handcuffs. The headline leaped off the page.

LOCAL GRAD STUDENTS CRACK GAMBLING RING

My jaw dropped. "Local grad students? You're giving me and Cal credit?"

"You guys solved it. Heck, I halfway considered giving you a byline. All my intel came from you." TJ took a deep breath. "I know we've had our differences, but you earned

the credit for this. I still don't know how you figured everything out."

I pretended to puff on a pipe. "It's elementary, my dear
Watson."

"You know Holmes never said that."

"Yes. I thought we were having a moment." Turning, I
went behind the register and spread the paper over the
counter.

*When an unnamed source tipped me off about a potential gambling
scheme at the local racetrack, I never dreamed that it might lure me
into a tangled web of intrigue and murder.*

I glanced up at him. "A tale of intrigue and murder?"

"Good, huh?" He beamed.

"A little over-written," I teased.

"Whoa there, Aly. Don't gush. People might think we're
becoming friends."

"Unlikely," I said dryly. Then I smiled.

This world wasn't the one I remembered. This TJ seemed
capable of growth. We didn't need to be at odds.

I returned to the article.

*After a cursory investigation, a local graduate student was enlisted
to go undercover and acquire more information.*

Or maybe not. "You enlisted my aid? This was all your
idea?"

"Well, I told you about the gambling ring, which helped
break the case."

"After I'd already found most of the evidence."

He shrugged. "My way makes for a better story."

"Uh-huh. Did you single-handedly disarm Jacob and save
the day, too?"

WHEN I ARRIVED home that afternoon, Cal was waiting on the front porch. One look at his face told me I wouldn't like whatever he had to say.

"This is a nice surprise," I said, trying to control my growing dread. "Do you want some coffee?"

"No, thanks." The haggard look in Cal's eyes broke my heart. We'd known each other for almost two years, and never had I seen him look this upset. "I was wondering if we could go for a walk."

"Absolutely. Where are we going?"

Instead of answering, Cal gestured ahead of me, down the sidewalk. I led the way until we reached the corner. He still hadn't spoken.

"I'm sorry about Jacob," I said to break the ice.

"Yeah."

We walked in silence for a while. Cal would tell me whatever he wanted to say when he was ready. We made it four blocks before he broke the silence. "Practically since we met, you've been solving murders. I bring you snacks while you're fighting crime and listen to you mull over potential solutions. You're the crime-fighting superhero, and I'm your supportive boyfriend. Nothing more than window dressing."

"You're much more than background to me," I said.

He held up one hand. "Let me finish. You're smart, you're capable, and I've always known you can handle yourself. Between your powers and your self-defense classes, I tricked myself into believing nothing could harm you."

Suddenly, I understood. Cal hadn't been close to my prior investigations. Even knowing I'd found killers before, this time he'd gotten a front-row seat.

"I'm so sorry. I'll never investigate another murder," I swore. Um, after I finished Penny's case. "I don't want to endanger anyone again."

"Don't make promises you won't keep." His eyes looked haunted. "I want you to use your powers to help others. Didn't you say you have an obligation?"

"My mom says that. Our powers are a gift, and using them for good is a thank you," I said. "But endangering people I love doesn't qualify as 'for good' in my book. I'm so sorry."

"Don't apologize again. I asked you to help. I practically begged. And I'm the one who got kidnapped."

"That wasn't your fault!"

"No, and it wasn't yours, either. That's not it. I don't want you to give up your life." He took a deep breath. "But I'm not sure I can be a part of it anymore. I need some time away."

Tears welled in my eyes. "What are you saying?"

"Last spring, Professor Ng offered me a research position for the rest of the summer. In South America."

I stared at him, rendered speechless. Professor Ng ran the botany department at our college. Several months ago, he'd listed a job for a research assistant deep in the rainforests. Between the play and the murder, I hadn't given the posting much thought. Plants and the outdoors weren't my thing. But Cal loved them.

"Why didn't you take it?" I asked.

"Things were so rocky after Christmas. We'd finally gotten onto firm footing. The last thing I wanted was to leave you."

"I had no idea," I whispered. The thought of him putting his career on hold for our relationship nauseated me. "Why didn't you tell me?"

"You would've told me to go."

I nodded and took a deep breath. "Absolutely. That's a once-in-a-lifetime opportunity!"

"That's the thing," he said. "Professor Ng emailed me yesterday. There's more work than expected. He could use another assistant."

His words punched me in the gut. "Y-you're going to South America for the rest of the summer?"

"Not just the summer. It's a full semester. I'll get credits, and the research will help with my dissertation."

My heart skipped a beat. After all we'd been through, I hated losing him, especially like this. But I couldn't ask him to stay. "Cal, that's an amazing opportunity. You have to go."

While it killed me to say the words, I meant them. This job would've been a dream for any grad student. I'd have encouraged him to take it last spring if I'd known.

Now, Cal had just found out his favorite cousin and life-long friend was a murderer who hated him. My inability to solve Morgan's death almost got him killed. He was a scientist, not a crime fighter. Learning that the gambling ring had taken him hostage was one of the worst moments of my life. I could only imagine how scared Cal had been. He was safer in the jungle.

Despite my promise, we both knew this wouldn't be the last case I investigated. At the moment, I was up to my elbows in Tripp's case file. If Tripp didn't kill Penny, once again, I'd be looking for a murderer.

As long as I had these visions, I'd be putting my loved ones in danger. Kevin, Katrina, even Olive had skills of their own. I'd often suspected my ex had powers, too, like his mother. They all understood. Cal was a regular person who could have a normal life without me. I couldn't give up the visions even if I'd wanted to.

He nodded. "I'm leaving tomorrow. I just came to say goodbye."

Tears streamed down my face. "When will you be back?"

"End of December." He pulled me into his arms. "I'll miss you."

Shutting my eyes, I laid my head against Cal's chest while trying to memorize how it felt to be held by him. "I'll miss you more."

Long distance was rough under the best of circumstances. Leaving after such a traumatic experience didn't bode well for our future. Maybe a few months apart would give me some much-needed perspective. I wanted to believe we'd work things out, but my brain knew the truth.

As much as I wanted to say we'd fix our relationship, I couldn't form the words. Cal truly would be better off without me.

"From the day we met, I knew you were something special," he said. "I never thought I'd be the one to end our relationship."

I sniffled and stepped away. "I understand."

"I should go. My flight's first thing tomorrow, and I haven't packed."

"Do you want me to drive you to the airport?"

He shook his head. "No, Mom's going to take me. I'm sorry, Aly."

"Me, too."

As I watched him walk to his car, emptiness and loneliness settled around me like a cape. When Cal and I met, he'd been everything I'd wanted in a boyfriend. Our friends called us "Calvyn" because we blended so well into one entity. Or we used to. Since Christmas, we'd had a lot of ups and downs. I thought we'd managed to come out stronger. But my life had become too dangerous for him. I hated it, but I couldn't change who I was. Cal wouldn't want me to.

The minute his car pulled away from the curb, Rusty walked outside. He slung an arm around my shoulder. "Want me to slash his tires? I know a guy."

I didn't ask how he knew. Between the fact that Cal never entered the house and our body language, my PI best friend put the pieces together even before seeing the tears streaking down my face.

"Is the guy you?" I asked.

"I can neither confirm nor deny."

I shook my head and leaned in, wrapping my arm around Rusty's waist. "No. He's right."

He kissed the top of my head. "Everything will be okay.

Listen, this may not be the best time, but the Saratoga prison called. You've been cleared to visit."

A wan smile crossed my face. "Tripp's spent more than twenty years in prison for a crime he may not have committed. There's no better time."

"That's my girl. You're going to be okay," Rusty said. "Also, I heard Manuel Diaz is looking for volunteers for his mayoral campaign…"

Although the last thing I cared about at the moment was who became our next mayor, I forced myself to sound enthusiastic. "Now you're talking! Sign me up."

We walked toward the house. Losing myself in work might be the way to mend my broken heart.

WHAT HAPPENS WHEN AN ATTACK ON A MAYORAL CANDIDATE ROCKS THE TOWN? FIND OUT IN ELECTION SEER

Coming soon!

# AUTHOR'S NOTE

Each book takes a village, and I upload each final version feeling extremely grateful to a host of people. There's my amazing cover designer, Victoria Cooper at LaVoisin, of course. No one other than my friends would pick up my books if not for her gorgeous artwork. And Madz Skills, the editor who notices so many little mistakes in each draft, I can't believe she hasn't fired me yet. Thank you to Jane Litherland for your expert proofreading. And while this is an ebook rather than audio, I want to thank Liza Jacob for the amazing job I know she'll do bringing this story to life.

*A Run for the Mystic* is the eighth Shady Grove Mystery, but it's the eleventh full-length cozy mystery I've published since 2021 and the thirteenth total. It's part of an extremely ambitious project I sometimes wish I hadn't taken on—a second six book story arc where Aly solves another decades-old murder. Theoretically, anyway. Shortly after beginning to draft this book, I started to think that I'd bitten off more than I could chew. Unfortunately, I couldn't decide not to finish it because I left readers hanging at the end of The Psychic's the Thing. But Melissa Erin Jackson made me realize that I am good enough, I am smart enough, and doggone it, I can write a series people will enjoy.

I was about to chuck this book out the window and walk away roughly seventeen thousand times over the past few months. Every time, Melissa pulled me back from the ledge. She listened with the patience of a dozen saints as I cursed everyone from myself to the guy who invented books. She listened, made me laugh, and helpfully distracted me when needed. Without Melissa, this series might have ended with Book 7 (which, truly, is an awful place to end a series. What kind of jerk would write a cliffhanger and never return?).

Thank you also to Carly Winter for actually having horse knowledge and pointing out everything I got wrong. (It was a lot.) If you find more mistakes, they are 100% my fault. Also thanks to Rebecca Douglass for your feedback and to Rosie Pease, Ellen Jacobson, and Gwen Gardner for your never-ending support and also looking at 700 versions of this cover.

2024 has been a tough year, but friends like these make everything better. Every day, I am extremely grateful to have found all of you.

# GET A FREE NOVELLA!

IF YOU SIGN up for my newsletter, you'll get *Mystic Treasure,* the story when Aly meets Emma. A little gift from me to you, because I appreciate my readers.

After a busy winter of murder-solving, Aly can't wait to relax with some family fun at the Shady Grove Annual Treasure Hunt. For twenty-five years, town residents have searched futilely for a chest containing the deed to an abandoned mansion on the edge of town. At this point, Aly's pretty sure the treasure is a myth, but she's always up for Shady Grove shenanigans.

When the Treasure Hunt gets underway, a suspicious new resident throws everything into question. Someone's got a hidden motive for participating, and the town may be in danger. Can Aly solve the mystery to save the day?

## Chapter 1

TODAY WAS the perfect day to win a fortune. I wasn't the only one who thought so: The Shady Grove Town Square hummed with excitement. Fluffy white cumulus clouds peppered the sky. Between the slight breeze and the mercury topping out at seventy degrees, this was the kind of gorgeous summer day that made it worth living through the humidity and thundershowers.

Half the town must have turned out to watch this event. Granted, half the town meant a few thousand people, but still. Town Square was bursting at the seams. Set near the end of Main Street, the largest park in town ran a block down to Second Street, with the other end across the street from City Hall. My three-year-old nephew and I stood under a tree, soaking it all in while we waited for my brother to join us.

Thankfully, Kyle hadn't yet seen the guy making balloon animals. On the corner nearest me, a marching band warmed up their instruments, complete with a bagpipes player. Town residents milled around, visiting the booths that had been set up to feed and entertain us. A huge banner extended across the square, welcoming everyone to the "WALTER SPARROW ANNUAL MEMORIAL TREASURE HUNT".

According to the rumor mill, Walter Sparrow was some eccentric millionaire who died about twenty-five years ago. Instead of leaving his money to a relative or a friend or a local animal shelter, he created this big annual party for everyone to try to win the big prize. No one had managed yet. My best friend Rusty suspected the entire story was a lie, and Walter just wanted to make sure we all talked about him forever after he passed.

Considering the amount of money supposedly on the line, I was surprised there weren't fortune hunters sniffing around all year, but Shady Grove wasn't like other towns. Maybe the same forces that led to unusual happenings kept outsiders away?

Or maybe our town was so tiny that no one outside a fifty-mile radius had heard of Shady Grove or old Walter? That was more likely.

Personally, I suspected Rusty was right. The whole thing

sounded like an urban legend. An excuse for a big summer party, but anyone expecting to find treasure would be sorely disappointed. Still, we'd teamed up and gotten ready for action. The practice solving clues should come in handy once Rusty finished getting his PI license.

Tugging my hand, Kyle peered up at me with his big brown eyes and heart-shaped face from beneath his adorably oversized sun hat. "What's a treasure hunt, Aunt Aly?"

I resisted smoothing an errant chestnut curl that was so like mine. "It means Rusty and I are going to follow clues to find a lost item that has been hidden somewhere in the town."

"I find it! What did Rusty lose?" Kyle asked.

I grinned at the spark of excitement in his eyes and smoothed a curl off of his forehead. My nephew had been born with the power to find lost objects, a secret we preferred to keep from the rest of the world as long as possible. Psychic powers ran in our family, but we'd recently learned that some people wanted to exploit what he could do. "Thanks, Little Man, but this game is for adults only. Besides, in a game, it's not fair to use our special abilities to win."

"Cheating?"

"Yes, that's considered cheating."

"Oh. I won't cheat." Kyle stuck out his lower lip. Then his gaze landed on one of the tables below the "WALTER SPARROW MEMORIAL TREASURE HUNT" banner. "Cookie?"

With a laugh, I let him drag me to the table, manned by my friend and the owner of the local coffee shop, Julie Capaldi. A self-described "recovering lawyer," Julie was a blue-eyed blonde who'd moved to Shady Grove a few years ago to take over her aunt's business. She'd set out cookies for sale, but also—and more importantly—iced coffee.

"Hey! Looking forward to the hunt?" she asked when we got within earshot.

"You know it," I said. "Rusty's excited to practice his PI

skills. I'm here to stop him from picking the locks of every store on Main Street."

She laughed. "He's going to be a great investigator. I miss having him at the cafe, though."

Until recently, Rusty had worked as the manager at On What Grounds?. After helping me learn to use my powers and solve a murder, my new best friend discovered his true calling. I often considered myself fortunate Julie hadn't banned me from her store when he left. Where would I get my coffee?

Then again, I suspected she had a thing for my brother.

"Hey, kiddo!" she said to Kyle before offering him a cookie. "You planning to hunt treasure today?"

"Aunt Aly said I was cheating."

My face flamed. Maybe she wouldn't understand him? Three-year-olds didn't have the best enunciation, and his mouth was full of cookie. I wasn't sure how much Julie knew, either about Kyle's abilities or mine. She certainly hadn't heard it from me, but small towns didn't have many secrets.

"Cheating? That's no good." She gave me one of those 'kids say the darnedest things' grins.

In response, I gave her the most innocent look I could muster. "We're learning new words this week. Anyway, are you entering?"

"No, I can't."

"Can't?"

She shook her head and laughed. "I did it last year. You're only allowed to enter once."

"That's odd," I said. "Kevin did it last year, too. I thought he wasn't entering because he wanted to spend the day with Kyle."

"That's part of it, I'm sure. But yeah, everyone gets one chance." She shrugged. "People with money are eccentric, right? It's Walter's estate, so he gets to make the rules. I'll send all my good vibes to you and Rusty."

At the mention of my partner, I turned to scan the crowd.

With the pre-hunt festivities drawing to an end, Town Square had cleared out somewhat. A lot of people still stood around, but most moved to ring the center, where the hunt would soon begin.

About fifteen feet away, I spotted my friend Tiffaneigh Pratt talking to Brad Stevens. The three of us studied science together at Maloney College. She still didn't want to admit they were dating, but the two of them looked awfully cozy. Their matching bright blue shirts with "WALTER SPARROW HUNTER" on the back told me everything I needed to know about their relationship—and my primary competition. Tiffaneigh hated to lose, and she had some flexible ideas about what constituted fair and legal gameplay.

We'd need to keep an eye on her if we wanted to win.

*Join my newsletter to get your ebook of Mystic Treasure today!*
*Or buy the audiobook*

# ALSO BY ADA BELL

**Shady Grove Psychic Mysteries**

Ever since 21-year-old Aluminum Reynolds moved to Shady Grove, New York, life has been full of surprises. Here's a list of Aly's adventures, in chronological order.

<u>Mystic Pieces:</u> Aly doesn't believe in psychics. Too bad she just had her first vision. Her first instinct is flat-out denial. After all, science and magic don't mix. But when a man is murdered, Aly realizes that she can use her strange new "gifts" to find the culprit. If she can avoid getting herself killed in the process.

<u>The Scry's the Limit</u>: Aly's just starting to get the hang of her psychic gifts when she literally stumbles over her favorite professor's body. She's devastated and determined to get justice. But with several people benefitting from Professor Zimm's death, how will Aly find the real culprit before they find her?

<u>Sight Seering</u>: As a psychic who gains powers from antiques, Aly is ecstatic to be invited to an estate sale. It's only after she arrives that she discovers the estate's owner didn't die in her sleep—she was murdered.

<u>Mystic Treasure</u>: Aly and Rusty are excited to participate in the annual Walter Sparrow Treasure Hunt. As the event gets underway, they realize that there's more to this event than meets the eye. Someone's got a hidden motive for participating, and the entire town may be in danger.

<u>Seer Today, Gone Tomorrow</u>: Just when Aly finally identified her sister-in-law's killer, they got away—and they're not alone. To make

matters worse, someone powerful has cursed the residents of Shady Grove. Aly's powers vanish. Without her psychic gifts, how will Aly find Katrina's killer and save the pet store?

The Pie in the Scry: After nearly a year, Aly's got a plan to bring Katrina's killer to justice. But before she and Kevin can implement it, she has a vision of someone murdering Tony, the bakery owner. As if that wasn't bad enough—the killer looks exactly like Aly.

Mystic Persons: Aly just completed the biggest spell she's ever attempted, with a little help. But the magic came with an unexpected side effect, and now she's got to figure out what happened to the dead man in the upstairs bath before her parents arrive for the holidays.

The Psychic's the Thing: At her roommate's urging, Aly tries out for the college play. She's surprised to be cast as understudy to the lead —but not nearly as shocked as when the star turns up dead.

A Run for the Mystic: Aly's thrilled to be invited to a VIP day at the track until a murder forces her to rein in the excitement. When the police blame her boyfriend's cousin, Aly must race to find the killer before an innocent man gets charged.

Election Seer: Coming soon!

8 Maids a-Meddling: When Aly's mom's best friend is found dead, they're sure the scene was staged. With the annal Holly Jolly Jamboree about to begin, they've got less than twenty-four hours to solve the murder before the killer disappears into the crowd.

**Haunted Haven Mysteries**

Emma thought life was weird before she found out she was a witch. Now she's got some pretty cool powers, a snarky-yet-insightful talking cat, and a fabulous mansion-turned-B&B, complete with ghost. Here is your complete guide to the *Haunted Haven* series.

Unfinished Witchness: Emma is thrilled to come into her legacy. Not only has she inherited stacks of money and a mansion, she's got magic! Everything is coming up roses until she finds her new chef dead in the kitchen and her other employee accused of murder. If she can't find the real killer, this haunted haven might never open for business.

Risky Witchness: Now that Emma's bed and breakfast is bustling with activity, she decides to treat herself to some R&R at the local fancy spa. But when she finds another guest dead, Emma becomes the prime suspect. She'll need the help of his ghost to help find the real killer before they find her.

Open for Witchness: When Ben convinces Emma to investigate the mysteriously closed bar in Shady Grove, she discovers it's being guarded by an extremely unpleasant spirit. The only way to help her friend is to solve the mystery—but the trail has been cold for decades. Can she close the case and reopen the bar?

Murder on the Witch Express: When Emma's romantic getaway turns deadly, she must find a killer before the train arrives at its destination and the murderer goes free.

**Bundles and Boxed Sets**

Shady Grove Psychic Mysteries 1-3

Shady Grove Psychic Mysteries 4-6

Haunted Haven Mysteries 1-3

# ABOUT THE AUTHOR

Ada Bell is an award-winning author who thought that it would be cool to use a secret identity when writing mysteries. After all, who doesn't want a secret identity? She doesn't remember where the idea for the Shady Grove mysteries started, but she freely admits that Kyle is based on a certain precious toddler in her own life. Ada loves Scooby Doo, superhero movies, STEM heroines, and cake. Mmm, cake.

Find Ada online at www.adabell.com, or get access to sneak peeks, news and more by joining her Facebook group, Ada Bell's Besties, or her mailing list.